SPECIAL MESSAGE TO READERS

This book is published by

THE ULVERSCROFT FOUNDATION

a registered charity in the U.K., No. 264873

The Foundation was established in 1974 to provide funds to help towards research, diagnosis and treatment of eye diseases. Below are a few examples of contributions made by THE ULVERSCROFT FOUNDATION:

A new Children's Assessment Unit at Moorfield's Hospital, London.

•

Twin operating theatres at the Western Ophthalmic Hospital, London.

•

The Frederick Thorpe Ulverscroft Chair of Ophthalmology at the University of Leicester.

•

Eye Laser equipment to various eye hospitals.

If you would like to help further the work of the Foundation by making a donation or leaving a legacy, every contribution, no matter how small, is received with gratitude. Please write for details to:

THE ULVERSCROFT FOUNDATION,
The Green, Bradgate Road, Anstey,
Leicester LE7 7FU. England
Telephone: (0533) 364325

Love is
a time of enchantment:
in it all days are fair and all fields
green. Youth is blest by it,
old age made benign: the eyes of love see
roses blooming in December,
and sunshine through rain. Verily
is the time of true-love
a time of enchantment – and
Oh! how eager is woman
to be bewitched!

ISLAND OF BLOSSOMS

For Karen it was the job of a lifetime: to catalogue a library on a Caribbean island. But her problems began at the beginning: she defies Laura, her employer, and Laura's son pays her unwelcome attentions. Only Michael makes everything worthwhile. When Karen finds a will proving that Laura is not the owner of the library and that her husband died in suspicious circumstances, she hurriedly completes her task. But when her work is missing, she is blamed and made prisoner. And she finds herself drifting out to sea, wondering if she will ever see Michael again . . .

Books by Grace Driver
in the Ulverscroft Large Print Series:

RETURN TO BALANDRA
A DOUBTFUL PROSPECT

GRACE DRIVER

ISLAND OF BLOSSOMS

Complete and Unabridged

ULVERSCROFT
Leicester

First published in Great Britain in 1980

First Large Print Edition
published November 1991

British Library CIP Data

Driver, Grace
Island of blossoms.—Large print ed.—
Ulverscroft large print series: romance
I. Title
823.914 [F]

ISBN 0-7089-2530-8

Published by
F. A. Thorpe (Publishing) Ltd.
Anstey, Leicestershire

Set by Words & Graphics Ltd.
Anstey, Leicestershire
Printed and bound in Great Britain by
T. J. Press (Padstow) Ltd., Padstow, Cornwall

1

KAREN WARDE looked up at the dingy window, high above the closely packed book-cases, where the cold November wind and driving rain rattled and threatened its ancient frame.

She shook her head and got up from her chair to walk across to where her employer sat at his mahogany roll-top desk intently reading a letter and apparently quite unaware of impending disaster.

"Mr. Arnold," said Karen, positioning herself so that she could be sure of attracting his attention.

He looked up at her with a bemused expression in his pale blue eyes. "Umm?"

"Mr. Arnold," she repeated, "I'm afraid that old window won't stand much more of this awful wind."

"Eh? Umm. Eh? What was that you said?"

"It's the window, Mr. Arnold. It's leaking. The rain is coming in." Karen rushed to find a towel as she saw a trickle of water run down over the edge of the shelf and drip on to the floor. She must mop it up before it ran back under the shelf to the books. So many of them were valuable.

Her employer appeared unperturbed. Over the top of his steel-rimmed spectacles that rested askew on the end of his nose, he watched Karen with bright eyes, their piercing intelligence making the rest of him grey into insignificance.

Karen's mop of curly auburn hair shone like a beacon in the dimly lit interior of the bookshop. She did what she could with the towel then stood up, a slight impatience in her manner. "*You see what I mean?*" she demanded, exhibiting the sodden towel.

The old man's gaze lingered on her slim young figure, her long legs which made her look taller than average height, and her slender expressive hands. There was something about her that reminded him of a duck chick he had fostered when he was a small boy, and how it wouldn't ever stop quacking. He smiled in reminiscence, but Karen had no way of knowing the comparison he was making. She just stood there in front of him hoping he might come up with a practical idea for shielding the books from further damage. If she waited long enough, he'd surely make some comment.

In those waiting moments Karen wondered if her employer ever combed his hair, for it stuck up in soft wisps, giving him a slightly comical air.

Behind her, the window was still rattling and banging to an ever alarming degree. Mr. Arnold gave a cursory glance towards the window and said, "How would you like to go to the West Indies?"

Karen blinked, not quite sure she had heard properly.

The old man chuckled. "That surprised you, I'll bet."

"But . . . " Karen looked confused, her eyes still glancing around the bookshop and her mind still on the threatened books.

"Never mind the windows, young woman. Here, read this for yourself."

He handed her the letter he had been reading.

She accepted the cream deckle-edged sheet and read it carefully.

Tabara, Bucare, West Indies.

Dear Mr. Arnold,

You will, I know, be sorry to learn of the death of my husband, Arthur Hammond, who has been a customer of yours for many years. He passed away peacefully two months ago, after a long illness.

My reason for writing is to ask for your assistance concerning his library of four thousand books, most of which have been collected with your inestimable help and knowledge.

Unfortunately, it may be necessary to realise some of the assets pertaining to the estate, and in this connection I should be most grateful if you would send a representative from your firm to catalogue the whole library and thus enable a value to be set on the entire collection as it stands.

Naturally, I shall be pleased to meet whatever travelling costs are incurred, and perhaps you will be kind enough to suggest what sum should be paid to your representative on completion of the work.

I trust that you, yourself, are in good health.

Sincerely yours,
Laura Hammond.

Karen looked up from the letter, excitement and conjecture alternating in waves. The rain was still beating at the window and the water was still dripping on to the the floor, but somehow it did not seem so loud.

"Well?" Mr. Arnold was waiting for her reaction.

Karen's titian complexion went rosy and her hazel eyes shone. "I'd love to go. D'you think I could do it?"

"Let me see." Her employer looked down at his clasped hands as they rested on the desk. "Just how long is it that you've been working for me?"

"Two years."

He looked up at her. "Well?" he challenged, "d'you think you've learnt enough in that time to make a careful list of some four thousand books?"

She smiled and nodded. "How long would I be gone?"

"Work it out for yourself."

"It would take me about . . . let me see . . . I could catalogue about fifty a day . . . that would be eighty days. Add one or two days off . . . about three months?"

He nodded. "I'd say that was about right. But there would also be travelling time."

"Would I have to go by air?"

"How else would you propose getting there?"

"By sea." She smiled at him, well aware it was a throw of the dice, but she had nothing to lose.

"Hmm." Mr. Arnold drummed his fingers on his blotter. "It might be difficult to get you on a ship at short notice." He studied her carefully. "Are you afraid of flying?"

"I don't know. I never have. It's just that if I'm going to the West Indies at all, it would be very nice to go by ship." Her smile gave a hint of apology. "I could come back to England by air," she added, making it sound like a concession. She gave him time to consider her request by side-tracking the issue. "If I do go, Mr. Arnold, how will you manage the shop on your own?"

"I don't intend to." He looked up at her over his spectacles and gave her one of his banana smiles, so that Karen knew she was putting absolutely nothing over on him. "There's a young divinity student I know who might be glad of a temporary job. But there's no need for you to worry about things like that. You'll have quite enough to think about." He resumed drumming his fingers on his blotter, then said, "I'll see what can be done about a ship, but you'll have to go by air if I can't get a cancellation of some sort at this late date." He paused. "Then I'll write and say that you'll be going?"

"Yes, please."

"That's settled, then." He picked up the telephone, and by the end of the morning Mr. Arnold had contacted a banana-shipping company who could offer a berth.

Karen was allowed to leave early that

afternoon, and as she travelled on the subway, back to her bed-sitter, her mind was on sunny skies and warm tropical nights. When she left the subway and emerged onto the wet pavements, with her plastic raincoat slapping against her legs and the rain squelching over her shoes, she hardly heeded the weather.

Once she stepped into the doorway of a shop and glanced at some bikinis while she retied her scarf as a protection against the wind and driving rain, before she hurried on excitedly.

When she reached her destination she had to struggle against the wind to fit her key into the lock, and when she was inside the house she had to push hard against the door to close it.

Taking off her brown woollen hat, she shook her damp hair, but it only curled tight against her temples.

She was about to run up the stairs when her landlady appeared in the hall. "Is anything wrong, Miss Warde? You're back earlier than usual."

Karen smiled and shook her head. "Nothing except the weather, Mrs. Beddoes. It's *horrible*!" She continued to smile.

"I've just been told that I'm to go to the West Indies."

"A holiday?"

"Oh no. I'm going to catalogue a library."

"That should keep you busy."

"It's going to take about three months. Will you be able to keep my room as it is, please? I'll pay you, of course."

"I'm sure we can come to some arrangement," replied Mrs. Beddoes, genially. "Here give me that plastic thing. I'll put it over my drying rack in the basement."

Two weeks later, Karen walked up the gangway to board the *Camello*, a small banana-cum-cruise ship bound for Trinidad which accommodated about a hundred passengers.

Her employer had been meticulous about her arrangements for the trip, and as far as Karen could make out, he had forgotten nothing.

On reaching Trinidad, he told her, she would be met at the docks by someone called Warren Grant and her destination was the small island of Bucare which was situated very close to the mainland. Who

Warren Grant was she had no idea, but presumably he would transport her to Bucare.

A friendly steward showed her to a berth on B deck, a small outside cabin with a porthole.

The cabin had a small clothes closet, a shaded reading lamp over the bed, and above the dressing-table was an air-conditioning control panel. Folk weave curtains and bedspread were in soft browns and fawns, and the carpet a warm tomato red. Adjoining the cabin was a compact shower unit and lavatory.

Her luggage, she saw, had already been placed on a low stool. About to take off her camel-hair coat and start unpacking she changed her mind. Her unpacking could wait. She would go back on deck and watch proceedings; it would be a pity to miss anything, and it would be interesting to watch her fellow passengers.

As she walked along the corridors she noticed the faint aroma of fuel oil; it pervaded the whole ship. She would later discover that the smell was a characteristic of the *Camello* and in time she would hardly notice it.

As she passed the Purser's office he was standing in his booth with the passenger list set out before him. He smiled as Karen approached him.

"Good morning, Miss Warde. Can I help you?"

"Yes, I think you can," she replied, surprised at being addressed by name. "It's my first experience of sea travel. Have you any free advice to give me?" she smiled.

"Well," he replied, "shall I start by asking you if you are happy with your cabin."

Karen nodded. "It's fine." Her smile broadened. "What would you have done if I'd said I wasn't?"

He grinned. "Oh, I expect we should do our best to find a cabin more to your liking."

She laughed.

He tapped his lip with his pen. "I take it that you are travelling on your own."

"Yes."

"About the dining room. Would you like me to ask the head waiter to arrange for you to sit with a family?"

"No, thanks." She paused. "Haven't you

any tables for one?"

The purser looked at her steadily for a few seconds, then, inclining his head to one side, said, "You might be a little conspicuous. Would you mind that?"

She saw his eyes flicker towards her hair and she replied. "Not particularly, but I'll accept your recommendation."

"Would you like to sit at the Captain's table?"

"No, thank you. That would be throwing me in at the deep end."

"Well, how about my placing you at the Chief Engineer's table for this evening? He usually has about six or eight people with him. He's a friendly family man and will help to introduce you to the other passengers. Perhaps, tomorrow, you might like to make other plans."

"I see. Well, if that's what you recommend I'll give it a whirl."

As she walked away, the Purser said, "I hope you enjoy your voyage with us. You'll find the *Camello* quite an informal ship."

"Thanks," said Karen, raising a hand as she went on walking.

She made her way out onto the

starboard side deck, but a biting wind was coming in off the sea. She wrapped her coat closer, descended the companionway and walked through to the port side in the lea of the wind so that she was able to stand at the rail where the wind was blustery but less cold.

Suddenly the wind snatched at her blue silk scarf, and before she could grab it, it was floating downwards.

Karen looked down despairingly, deciding at once that there was no hope whatever of its recovery.

Then her attention was caught by a tall man with hair the colour of lightly browned toast. He was wearing a thick maroon sweater and slacks and was striding purposefully up the gangway with his eye on the errant scarf. He grabbed at it and held it aloft, searching the faces of those at the rail high above him.

For an instant Karen was immobile, and feeling rather foolish. She raised her arm in acknowledgement, but before she could speak, a voice beside her called out, "Michael!"

Karen concluded that he had not seen her own signal. Evidently the man recognised the girl standing beside her.

"Is this yours?" he called up. His voice affected Karen in a strange way. Her pulse quickened as she nodded and held on to the rail with both hands as if to steady herself.

The dark-haired girl beside her pointed to Karen and, turning to her, said, "I'll get it for you," and ran along the deck and down the stairs towards the embarkation point.

The moment had come and gone so quickly and yet the incident was to remain vivid in Karen's mind. The dark girl was lost to sight for only a few minutes. She reappeared with the scarf and handed it to Karen.

"Thanks," said Karen. "I'd have been sorry to lose it," she added, now tying it round her head and making sure that it did not escape a second time.

The girl beside her said, "My the wind's cold!"

Karen nodded. The girl was about her own age, or perhaps a bit older. "Never mind, we're headed for the sunshine."

The dark girl was watching her closely. "Your first visit to the West Indies?"

"How did you guess?"

The girl tipped back her short-bobbed head and laughed. The sound had a musical note. "It was the way you said, 'We're headed for the sunshine' I guess."

Karen did not reply. The girl seemed good-humoured enough, and yet she made her feel at a slight disadvantage in some way. Karen leaned forward on the rail and gave her attention to the activity below yet curiosity made her turn to look at her fellow traveller. She was difficult to assess, and her accent hard to place. "Are you an American?" she ventured.

The dark girl shook her head. "No. Creole . . . or if you want to be specific – originally of Spanish descent but ancestors settled in the West Indies in the sixteenth century." She cocked an eyebrow as she studied Karen's reaction.

"Oh." It was all Karen could think of to say.

The girl laughed. "By the way, my name is Frances. What's yours?"

"Karen. Karen Warde."

"I'm Frances Drake," she replied, holding up a hand. "No! Please don't say it . . . " she said, laughing, then added, "What absolutely gorgeous hair you have."

Karen tucked away a loose strand. "Actually, it's a nuisance. It's so curly I can never do much with it."

"But it's so ... oh, I don't know ... alive."

"It certainly has a life of its own," said Karen, laughing.

Frances said, "Incidentally, where are you sitting in the dining room?"

"With the Chief Engineer."

Frances pulled a face. "You won't have much fun there. Why don't you sit with us?"

"Who is *us*?"

"Myself and my husband."

Karen hesitated. "That's kind of you, but the Purser has already fixed me up for tonight. May I see how it works out?"

"By all means, but I can tell you – you'll be dead bored with the Chief Engineer. I know." She bent over the rail as something caught her interest.

They sailed with the tide at midnight.

Frances was right about Karen's table

companions, though to give the Chief Engineer his due, he was doing his best with an odd assortment of passengers. Unfortunately, almost his entire conversation consisted of platitudes, and in the intervals were jokes that only he thought were funny, doubtless from being repeated so often.

Karen found her attention wandering. The lady on her right was preoccupied with her soup, her spoon and the cord of her antiquated hearing aid – collectively a problem to her.

On Karen's other side a thin young man spoke in monosyllables, no doubt embarrassed into silence by the comments uttered in loud tones by his doting mother, seated on his left. Karen quickly decided that Frances was right and that for breakfast next morning she would move.

She glanced around the dining room, speculating on possibilities, and saw Frances waving to her from the far end, mocking her with an exaggerated flick of her wrist. Karen's spirits lifted.

She looked again at the table where Frances was sitting. She was with seven others at a round table, and seated next to her was a handsome dark man with broad shoulders and a suggestion of the square about him. Karen speculated on his occupation.

Then she happened to glance across at the captain's table and was surprised to see the man who had rescued her scarf. He was sitting beside the captain and they appeared to be having an animated discussion. Karen returned her attention to eating her second course, but an unbid shiver of excitement travelled up her spine.

The fresh salmon was delicious, and with it was a mixed salad such as she had never tasted, the exotic ingredients mixed with a creamy tangy dressing.

She made an effort to talk to the lady on her right who had now resolved the problem with the cord of her hearing-aid and was pleased for someone to take an interest in her. Karen listened. It was much the easier way, because each time she attempted to say anything her remark had to be repeated three times. Mrs. Bennet was her name, and she chattered on about her garden at home which she had left in someone else's care and was not at all happy about.

When the meal was over, Karen walked out with Mrs. Bennet and they parted company at the door of the library, a place which was to become a favourite haunt of Karen's.

She browsed along the shelves and found a copy of *Gone With The Wind.* She had seen the film but had never read the book. It would do nicely for the voyage.

She then made her way to the main lounge, found a quiet corner and started to read, but almost as soon as her interest was engaged, there was a tap on her shoulder. She looked up to see Frances standing beside her, accompanied by the handsome dark man, who towered above her.

They both sat down, one on either side of her. Karen closed her book.

After introducing her husband, Frances explained that Giles was a forestry officer and that his job took him to many different islands in the Caribbean.

Karen was very taken with Giles, especially his voice, which had a deep mellow timbre and, to Karen, an even more unusual accent than Frances. Later on, she discovered that it was Bajan . . . he came from the island of Barbados.

"How long have you . . . ?" But Karen got no further with her question because Giles leapt up at the sight of the tall tousle-headed man who had recovered her lost scarf. He was swinging his way across the lounge towards them.

Giles went forward to greet him, shaking his hand. "Frances told me she saw you coming on board."

The newcomer, now wearing a brown tweed jacket and corded slacks, grinned in a slow, warm way, and Karen's heart did a flip, though he did not appear to notice her until the enthusiasm of the meeting had subsided and Frances got a chance to introduce her.

"Karen, this is Michael. Michael Williamson," she said.

"Hello," said Karen, looking into a pair of serious grey eyes which were so clear she involuntarily dropped her gaze for an instant.

Michael Williamson nodded perfunctorily and resumed his conversation with Giles, though Frances insisted on bombarding him with questions whenever she got the chance.

Suddenly, Frances turned to Karen and said, "You know, Michael lives on a tiny island just off the coast of Trinidad – somewhere most people have never even heard of."

"What's the name of it?" asked Karen, more out of politeness than anything.

"Bucare." Frances smiled her best know-it-all smile and said, "There, you're no wiser than before, are you?"

"Well, actually," replied Karen quietly, "that's where I'm going."

There was a stunned silence. All three of them looked at her. Frances opened her eyes very wide and said, "Whatever for?"

"Frances!" cut in Giles. "I really think you are going too far."

"Sorry. But I can't possibly imagine what there is to do on Bucare apart from spending a very quiet holiday. There's nothing there except one or two large houses in the hills and a tiny settlement round the bay."

"Then I'll keep you in suspense," said Karen, playfully.

Whether it was the knowledge that Karen was on her way to Bucare, she never knew, but at that moment Michael Williamson excused himself and walked quickly away and disappeared through the doorway leading out on deck. Giles followed.

"Why do you have to be so secretive?" huffed Frances. "What are you going to Bucare for, anyway?"

"To catalogue a library," replied Karen. She began to feel edgy and there was the unmistakable feeling of electricity in the air. "I'm sorry, Frances. I didn't mean to be awkward."

Frances shrugged and said, "That's okay," but her manner was cool.

In an effort to resume a friendly note, Karen asked the question she had started to ask before. "Have you known Michael Williamson a long time?"

Frances nodded. "He and Giles were at school together in Barbados."

"And what about you?"

"Oh, I went to Barbados, also, but on the opposite side of the island."

"Does Michael Williamson work for the Forestry Commission?"

"Goodness, no. He farms sugar cane," she replied, giving Karen a sly glance.

Frances made the excuse that she ought to find Giles and left. Karen picked up her library book and idly turned the pages. She was restless, now, and somewhat uncomfortable. She felt in the wrong yet was puzzled as to why. It was obvious she had put a foot wrong and was embarrassed that she had been so ill-at-ease when Michael Williamson appeared on the scene. She wished, now, that she had been more forthcoming about her reason for going to Bucare, but Frances, with her know-it-all manner, had piqued her into reticence.

She made her way to her cabin intending to have an early night, but when she opened her cabin door and looked through the porthole and saw the pale November moonlight shining on a calm sea, she changed her mind. She would go for a walk on deck and get some air.

She put on her coat and buttoned it up to the neck, then put her blue scarf over her head and tied it under her chin, peasant style, which she had never liked doing very much but had to admit was the surest means of defence against any suggestion of wind. However, she need not have worried – the sea breeze had dropped considerably, and to her surprise there were quite a number of passengers walking the deck.

Though cold, the air was wonderfully fresh and she took deep breaths as she strode along. She was already discovering that there was a magical isolation about being at sea.

The wash of the water against the sides of the *Camello* lulled her into passivity and she rested her elbows on the rail, gazing out at the interminable expanse of water, clear and shining under the moon's beneficence. It was hypnotic. Then she looked down at the portholes on the lower deck where the light shone out onto the creaming wake.

About to walk on, she noticed a man standing at the ship's rail further along, and saw that it was Michael Williamson. His hands were deep in the pockets of his duffle coat. She hesitated, not wanting to pass him, but just as she was about to retreat he saw her. If she turned now it would appear as if she was pointedly avoiding him, so she walked on.

As she walked past him, he spoke. "Hello, again," he said, quite non-committally.

"Hi, there," she replied, as nonchalantly as she could. "What a beautiful night this is."

"Yes. Most unusual for November, this far north. No cloud at all. I don't ever remember seeing the sea quite like this."

"You've done this trip before?"

"Many times."

"On this particular ship?"

"Not always. But the *Camello* is my first choice. I know the crew well by now."

For a moment or two neither of them spoke. Karen wanted to bring up the subject of her destination, but was unsure of his reaction. He must have sensed her predicament, for he said, "So, you are going to Bucare."

"Yes." Eager to impart information that would convince him of her friendliness, she added, "to catalogue a library."

"I see. I must admit it crossed my

mind to wonder what possible reason there could be."

"Perhaps you know the place. It's called *Tabara.* A Mrs. Hammond owns it, I believe."

Michael Williamson thrust his hands even deeper into his pockets and took a deep breath. "Yes, I know *Tabara,*" he replied.

There was something in the tone of his voice that cautioned Karen to say no more, and yet her curiosity was far from satisfied. She left the subject, temporarily, asking him how long the voyage to Trinidad would take.

"About twelve days, usually." He paused and looked up at the moon. "The wind could change later in the night."

"Does that mean a rough sea?"

"More likely choppy. But it won't be long before we're in warmer waters." He turned to look at her. "Is this your first sea trip?"

Karen nodded, silent now, waiting for a lead so that she might question him further about Bucare. His reluctance to discuss *Tabara* was, perhaps, something personal, but surely there was no harm in asking about the island in a general way. She said, tentatively, "Could you tell me something about Bucare? How large an island is it?"

He laughed. "How small, I think you mean."

"How small, then?"

"About five square miles."

"Do many people live there?"

"At an optimistic guess I would say, fifty, sixty, perhaps." He turned to look at her in the bright moonlight. "What were you expecting?"

"I'm not expecting anything. I'm just naturally interested in where I'm going," she replied, rather put out.

Michael Williamson continued to scrutinise her closely and Karen felt a momentary shiver. Her hands went to her coat collar and she turned it up as if to protect herself.

"Are you cold?" He was mildly concerned.

"No," she replied. "But I think I'll carry on round the deck before I go down to my cabin."

"Then I'll bid you goodnight." He barely moved.

"Goodnight, Mr. Williamson," she replied, formally, as she walked away.

She had almost reached the companion-way when he called after her. "One moment, Miss Warde."

She hesitated, turning in surprise and waiting until he caught up with her.

"Are you quite sure you wouldn't like me to tell you more about Bucare?"

"I had rather hoped you would, but it doesn't matter. I can find out for myself . . . when I get there." Then she walked down the steps to B deck to locate her cabin, unreasoned anger snapping at her heels.

2

THE following morning Karen awoke with a strange feeling in the region of her solar plexus. For a moment or two she lay still, remembering where she was, but when she tried to sit up and looked towards the porthole, something odd was going on . . . a bank of grey cloud was zooming in a diagonal fashion, first one way and then the other.

She hastily flopped down again. She could feel the ocean swell and her stomach heaved with it. Sea-sickness had taken her completely by surprise.

She tried again to sit up, but she had to close her eyes and lie down again. Lying down was easier and after a few desperate minutes she turned her face to the wall and tried to doze off again.

Some time later she awoke drowsily, aware that someone was standing beside her bunk and laughing. "Poor baby," said Frances.

"Go away! It's not funny," she retorted in a small voice. It annoyed Karen that Frances should be amused at her plight. Why wasn't *she* seasick, anyway?

"I've turned on the air-conditioning," said Frances, brightly. "That ought to help a bit. Didn't you bring any travel sickness pills with you?"

"I never thought of it," groaned Karen.

"Silly girl. I'll go and get you one – though it's a bit late now. It might even make you worse. You should have taken one before we sailed."

"How I hate know-alls." grumbled Karen aloud to herself when Frances had gone. But she knew in her heart that she envied Frances just a little. She had obviously travelled a lot and her experience put Karen at a disadvantage. Frances had so much confidence it was mortifying. Smug, in fact, that's what she is, she decided. Perhaps being married makes a difference, though I really can't see why it should. Her thoughts wandered, lost in sympathy for her own discomfort.

It was the stewardess, and not Frances, who returned.

"I met Mrs. Drake in the corridor,"

she said. "She told me you were feeling poorly. Is there anything I can do for you?" She sounded sympathetic.

"I think I must be seasick. It's horrible. It feels as if a kipper is stuck half way down my throat."

The stewardess smiled. "That's about it. I know it's awful while it lasts, but you'll soon get acclimatised. Not only that, but the further we get across the Atlantic the more the weather will improve." She went into the bathroom and half filled a beaker of water, then feeling in her white coat pocket, she produced two foil-wrapped tablets. "Here, take this one. It will help you sleep. I'll leave the second pill here on the bedside table in case you need it later on."

"Thanks," said Karen, gratefully clutching at the beaker and swallowing the tablet. "It was good of you to come in and see me."

"It's my job to look after you, Miss Warde." She paused. "I'll pop in again later just to make sure you are all right. Try and get some sleep now."

Karen barely had the will to reply, but she gave a watery smile and turned her face to the wall. But that was no good. She could feel the engines vibrating, so she lay on her other side and gazed out through the porthole at the dark sky which kept moving up and down. "Ugh," she said, aloud. Then closing her eyes she drifted into an uneasy sleep as the pill began its work.

She awoke later that evening and took the other pill the stewardess had left for her, then slept right through the night, unaware that the stewardess had looked in on her.

In the morning she surfaced in a stupor and attempted to sit up, but it was no good, she still felt groggy.

The stewardess entered with a light breakfast on a tray, but Karen waved it away. "Sorry. I just can't bear the thought of food." She flopped back on her pillows again, only too thankful to lie there.

"I think it would make you feel better to drink a cup of tea. Try. You can just about manage to drink it lying down if I put another pillow behind your head."

Karen nodded and made the effort. The stewardess was right. It did help a little.

Frances paid a couple of quick visits

and made sympathetic noises which did not altogether ring true, but all Karen wanted was to be left alone until the sea grew calmer.

It was three whole days later when she awoke to find that her sea-sickness had vanished as quickly as it had come. She sprang out of bed and went to look out of the porthole.

It was just getting light and she could see a pale blue sky. The sun was peeping above the horizon and prisms of light were catching the spray as it swept the porthole. Gone was the high swell and the sea was making a gentler sound as it lapped the sides of the ship and winged into white foam. It was really good to feel alive again.

She looked at her watch. Six o'clock. She was hungry now, but it was too early for breakfast.

She opened her closet and selected a pale blue linen sleeveless dress and tossed it on to the bed, then went into the bathroom. The shower felt good but her hair got wet. Bother, she thought, that's something else I didn't bring — a shower cap. Perhaps they'll have one at the shop. Anyhow, I might as well wash my hair now. It will freshen me up.

When she had showered and dried her hair, she dressed. Then slipping a warm white jacket around her shoulders she emerged from her cabin. All was quite and she met no-one as she made her way along the corridor past the Purser's office and out through the swing doors on to the deck.

The air was wonderful and she took deep breaths standing at the rail. There seemed to be nobody else about, but just when she began to think the ship was deserted she heard the sound of splashing. Someone was in the swimming pool and she went to investigate. But when she saw who it was she turned and walked the other way. She did not feel up to meeting Michael Williamson at that hour of the morning, and especially as he was alone. There was something much too intimate in meeting a man in his bathing trunks, alone, at six o'clock in the morning.

She wandered to the other end of the ship and stood at the prow watching the bows cut through the aquamarine water as the snowy spray spread fast and wide on either side.

The air was purer than any she had ever breathed and a sense of well-being filled her, which made her think once again of breakfast.

There was a light tap on her shoulder. It startled her. "Oh! It's *you*!"

"That's right. Who did you think it was?" Frances was dressed in white polyester slacks, an Italian styled flowered tunic and pale leather sandals. She looked elegantly casual and very comfortable. "Are you feeling better this morning?"

"Yes, thanks. It was nice of you to let the stewardess know."

"Don't mention it. That's what she's there for." She gave Karen a straight look. "By the way, have you decided to sit with us this morning?" She was as provocative as ever.

Karen nodded. Then she laughed. "I hate you for being so right. That poor Chief Engineer was rather a bore, poor man. But I suppose he has been doing the same thing for so long it has become automatic for him to keep conversation going along well defined paths."

"You're learning fast, mon enfant," flashed Frances as they entered the dining room.

Giles, already seated at the same round table, looked up and smiled. Karen sat opposite him and Frances took a chair beside her husband.

"Been for a swim already?" commented Giles. His eyes betrayed amusement.

Karen shook her head. "I forgot to bring a shower cap and ended up washing my hair." She laughed. "Though I might be tempted tomorrow, now that I know where to find the pool."

Ten minutes later Michael Williamson joined them. He looked across at Karen quite casually and said, "How's the sea-sickness?"

"Completely gone," replied Karen. "Thank goodness. It was perfectly horrible whilst it lasted."

"With luck you may not ever be afflicted with it again. It often happens." He looked at her critically and was about to say something, but instead he picked up the breakfast menu and studied it, frowning.

Frances said, "You haven't told us what you've been doing in England."

"Just a quick visit," replied Michael, non-committally and continuing to study the menu.

Giles glanced at Frances and saw that she was biting her lower lip. "I didn't mean to pry," she said. "Sorry."

Karen felt called upon to say something. She quickly asked Frances if she would show her where the shops were.

"You mean shop. There is only one." She paused. "Okay. I want to see what they have to offer, anyway."

Breakfast was finished in comparative silence and when they were through, Karen and Frances excused themselves.

Michael turned to Giles. "Sorry if I sounded terse. I didn't want to explain my business in front of the other girl. You had better explain to Frances that I have just returned from Iceland."

"Frances always sounds nosy," explained Giles, "but she doesn't mean to be. She's just intensely interested in everything and everybody."

"I should know that by now. Forget it." He paused. "Incidentally, what takes the red-headed girl to Bucare? Do you know?"

"No, I don't. But I'll bet Frances does by now. Want me to ask her?"

Michael shrugged. "Not on your life. My query might be misconstrued and that would never do."

With a hundred passengers on board, life on the voyage became very social. The weather continued to be perfect, there was plenty of entertainment and people were friendly. Frances was very good company in small doses, and Giles never resented Karen being part of a threesome.

Michael Williamson appeared reluctant to make up a foursome. He was apparently more interested in mixing with the Captain and the crew.

Karen would have liked to take advantage of an early morning swim in the pool, but she lacked the courage, afraid of meeting up with Michael Williamson because he had made it fairly obvious that he was not interested in her at any price. It would have been different if other people had used the pool at the same time, but they never appeared on the scene until after breakfast. Karen settled, instead, for a leisurely stroll to the prow, as she had done on her first morning when her sea-sickness had left her. Sometimes Frances would join her, but Frances was unpredictable, and more often they would not meet until breakfast time.

After breakfast, the day swung into full activity, with deck games, cards, chess, horse racing and bingo. Even an occasional game of scrabble. Sometimes a film, and quite often there was dancing.

The voyage meant a thoroughly enjoyable holiday for Karen. She benefited from the sun and sea air and was soon glowing with health.

She was surprised and pleased to discover that she had developed a tan, and yet she had never risked direct sunlight because whenever she did so her delicate fair skin always burned. Frances explained that the sea breezes and reflected light had done the trick, which meant that she had avoided the ultra-violet rays.

Karen asked Frances's advice on how she should protect her skin on Bucare.

"Oh," replied Frances, somewhat airily, "I shouldn't think you'll have any problem . . . so long as you avoid the sun at midday. The humidity acts as a guard, too, but you mustn't overdo it."

Karen did not encounter Michael until several more days had passed, but she often saw him in the distance, both in the dining room at the captain's table and also on deck, and always in the company of men.

She had seen him with Frances and Giles once or twice, though not as often as she would have expected since they were supposedly old friends. He certainly never came to sit with them if she herself was present. Could it be that he was avoiding her because he knew she was going to Bucare?

She occasionally caught the sound of his pleasantly modulated voice, which affected her more than she cared to admit. But not once did she glance openly in his direction. She was very much attracted to him, to her annoyance, yet at the same time aggravated by the way he kept his distance. She had sensed him looking at her sometimes, but she carefully avoided meeting his gaze.

The following morning, when breakfast

was over, Karen sauntered along to the ship's library. She wanted to return *Gone With The Wind.* For some reason she couldn't get going on it, perhaps because it was such a long book and she knew she would not be able to finish it by the end of the voyage. She was not in the mood for the classics and turned to lighter reading. She picked up Longfellow's *Hiawatha* and smiled to herself; it had long been a favourite and she had never tired of the exciting rhythms it excited as one read it – like the music of a mountain stream as it tumbles from pebbles and rocks on its downward tumble.

She chose a quiet corner and starting reading and before she realised it, became totally immersed. Two hours later Frances came looking for her.

"So that's where you've got to! No wonder we couldn't find you. What are you reading?" She gave *Hiawatha* a cursory glance and laughed. "We did that at school," she said, dismissively.

Karen was unperturbed. "Why were you looking for me?"

"We're waiting for you to play deck tennis."

"*Must I!*" Karen pulled a face.

"Yes. You must. Come and be sociable."

"All right. I'll meet you up there. I want to pop this book along to my cabin first."

Frances nodded and was gone. Karen went to her cabin and a few minutes later, reluctantly joined the others.

Although she kept *Hiawatha* on her bedside table for reading at night, she continued to make a habit of visiting the library after dinner.

One evening, when she was sitting there alone in her usual corner, three men sauntered in. She looked up from her book and saw that they intended settling down to play cards. It was the Captain, and with him were the Chief Engineer and a young fresh-faced officer she had not seen before.

Karen picked up the book she was reading and got up to go. The Captain smiled at her. As she returned his smile she went towards the door not noticing that someone was coming in. The man coming in put out his arms to prevent her stumbling. It was Michael Williamson.

"You'll have to watch where you're

going, Miss Warde!" His tone was jocular.

Karen flushed. "And so will you, Mr. Williamson," she retorted, her eyes glinting. She was furious with herself for being so careless as not to see him coming. She saw the other men smile and felt chagrin that they had heard her speak so sharply. She was certainly not sharp by nature, but there was something about Michael Williamson that provoked her.

As she hurried along the corridor she determined it would not happen again. She would make doubly sure of her actions in future. The night before they reached Trinidad the captain gave a gala evening, and now that the ship was into perfect weather the dancing went on deck. The crew spent the day fitting extra lights and hanging bunting, and now there was an air of festivity.

Karen decided she would wear her long dress. It was the palest apple green, and against her gleaming red hair and recently acquired tan she was pleased with her image as she looked in the mirror before leaving her cabin.

She wore no jewellery except her gold

bracelet watch, and her reflection told her that none was necessary. Not that it would have made any difference — she possessed no other jewellery.

As she entered the main lounge she could see that drinks were being served.

"What can I get you, Miss Warde?" Michael Williamson was as her side. She almost jumped with surprise at his approach.

"Thank you," she said. "I'd like a medium dry sherry."

She watched Michael Williamson thread his way through the chattering crowd to where the drinks were being dispensed. He was wearing a dinner jacket and looked immaculate — that is, except for his unruly sun-bleached hair. Yet that was part of his attraction. Karen tried to visualise what he would look like with smoothed down hair, and in her imagination found herself reaching out to touch it. She switched her mind away from the sensation as he walked back carrying their drinks.

"What have you got there?" she asked.

He held up his glass so that the amber liquid caught the light. "Scotch and ginger ale." He looked at her quizzically.

Karen, suddenly unsure of herself, looked around for Frances and Giles, and to her relief saw them coming towards them. They both had drinks.

Giles addressed Karen. "We have been looking everywhere for you. How long have you been here?"

"About five minutes."

"Which way did you come?" asked Frances.

Michael said, facetiously, "Oh, she just climbed the companionway, walked a few steps and, hey presto, here she was."

"Very funny," said Frances, petulantly.

Giles looked puzzled. "Are we all the same table for dinner?"

Karen said nothing.

"Why not," replied Michael. "After all, it's the last night." He turned to Karen. "I hope you have no objection, Miss Warde." A slightly sardonic smile played about his mouth.

"No objection at all, Mr. Williamson," she replied, somewhat archly.

"Oh, for god's sake! Can't you two get around to christian names?" Frances registered impatience and turned on her heel, leaving the other three to follow her.

It was after dinner. Frances and Giles had got up to dance and Karen half hoped that Michael would ask her to dance with him. Instead, he leaned towards her and said, "Shall we go somewhere where we can talk?"

Startled at his request, Karen replied, haltingly, "Y-yes. Of course. But what about?"

"Bucare."

"But I thought you made it plain you wanted to keep off the subject."

He did not reply but picked up her stole and placed it around her shoulders, so that she found herself accompanying him in spite of her inclination to resist. She was puzzled that he should have sought her out at this late stage of the voyage.

Michael led her to the rail of the ship away from the main concentration of passengers. He leaned over the side and looked down at the dark water, about to speak, but instead, he raised his head and looked out to sea where the moon now made a silver path to the horizon.

Then turning to face Karen and look her straight in the eyes, he said, "How long do you expect to stay on Bucare?"

"About three months. Why do you ask?"

"Just interest." He shrugged.

"I'm going there to catalogue a library," she said.

He looked surprised. "At *Tabara*, you say?"

"Yes. A Mrs. Hammond."

Michael looked down at the shimmering water and for a few moments there was silence between them. Finally, he said, quietly, "To catalogue a library is something I would never have guessed, meeting you for the first time. When you were reluctant to give your reason for going I wondered if perhaps you were going out there to be married."

"Whatever gave you that idea?"

"Oh, your standoffishness, I suppose. Every time I've tried to be sociable you've bitten my head off as if all males were obnoxious to you except those you can be sure won't make passes at you."

Karen was shaken. "Is that really your impression of me?" She was indignant.

"Well, it just shows how wrong you are. I've never been abroad before, and at the moment I am somewhat out of my depth. I certainly never intended to be standoffish. To be honest, I felt as if I'd got off on the wrong foot with you as soon as you knew I was going to Bucare. What *is* it about this mysterious island?"

Michael stood quietly. He waited for a few seconds then, as Karen started to move away he caught her arm. "Please don't go, Karen. I want us to be friends."

She lingered over the way he spoke her name. It was more of an endearment. She turned to look at him, and in spite of herself, she smiled.

"That's the first time you have smiled at me," he said. "Smiles for everyone else, but none for me."

Karen's hazel eyes softened, little gold flecks of light appeared in them. "Am I forgiven?" She was still smiling.

"I guess so." He grinned.

She was suddenly aware of his nearness. She turned to lean on the ship's rail.

"You're blushing," said Michael. "I like that. There are so few girls today who do."

"I'm afraid it makes me annoyed. It lets people know how I feel, too easily. I try hard not to, but it doesn't make any difference."

"Don't ever change," he said. "It goes beautifully with your hair."

Karen laughed. "Everybody teases me about my red hair. I think I'll have it cut whilst I'm on Bucare – all this length is a bit hot for the tropics."

"Please don't."

"I can't promise not to."

He turned to look out to sea again. "Now I'm interfering in your affairs. I have no right to do that. No right at all." He turned to face her.

Reaching out, he lifted her chin so that she had to look up at him. His eyes now were a deep grey-blue and drew upon her senses so that she almost lost her bearings. Then he took her hand and drew her into the shadows, caught her in his arms and before she realised what was happening he was kissing her. His lips were warm and firm and his kiss tender, though she was well aware that beneath the tenderness was an ardent nature.

The kiss lasted longer than she felt it

should. Her pulse was racing and her response to him all too revealing when she knew so little about him. She tried to pull away from his embrace but he was reluctant to let her go.

"Please," she murmured.

He relaxed his hold then, but as he let her go his hands moved down over her tingling bare arms, caressing them as he sought her hands. He lifted her fingers to his lips, and the feeling of joy the gesture gave her could not be denied. Karen knew instinctively how aware he was of how her skin yielded to his touch – it was impossible for her to control her physical response.

She turned away from him and leaned on the ship's rail. The breeze was like the touch of swansdown. She wanted to dance along the shining path to the horizon, but instead she looked down at the silvery wake as it swished and foamed. With Michael beside her, the sound of it held her spellbound. Michael's kiss and the magic of the night bore her on wings of bliss.

Michael leaned against the rail with his back to the sea and watched her.

She had the feeling he wanted her to turn and meet his gaze, but she found it impossible. She *must* find her bearings. Such a rush of emotion was new to her.

"So that's where you've got to!" The voice broke upon the silence. It was Frances. She and Giles were suddenly beside them.

Michael turned and said, non-committally, "Have you been looking for us?" There was no welcoming smile on his face.

Frances did not answer. Karen tried to read her expression but she looked away. Then, addressing Karen, she said in a clipped voice, "Too, too romantic, don't you think?"

Giles made no comment but began to talk to Michael about the ship's facilities.

Karen moved away and wandered into the saloon where some of the passengers had gone to listen to the orchestra. Frances followed her. "What have you and Michael been up to? You looked quite guilty when we found you."

Karen stopped and looked hard at Frances. "Guilty?" She frowned. "What an odd thing to say."

Frances looked sullen but made no rejoinder.

Karen puzzled, walked on. She found herself a seat close to the orchestra. Perhaps the music would silence Frances, and for the time being it did.

Giles and Michael joined them a while later, but there was little conversation. Somehow, Frances had put a damper on the easy companionship between the four of them, and it was not long before Karen and Michael found themselves alone again. However, Michael's manner had changed to formality now, and Karen knew that it had been Frances who had caused it. In an effort to recapture their former intimacy, she said, "I hear that you've known Frances and Giles a long time."

"Yes," replied Michael, somewhat off-handedly. "Years. Since school days." He did not elaborate and they both fell silent.

Finally Michael stood up, flexed his muscles and said, "I think I'll take a turn on deck before going to my cabin. Care to join me?"

Karen hesitated.

"Perhaps you are tired."

"It's not that," she replied hastily. Her thoughts were racing. She wanted to go with him, but remembering their shared moments before dinner, her courage deserted her. She wanted him to take her in his arms again and kiss her, and she wondered if he knew how she felt. Did such things *always* happen so quickly and easily on board ship? He had probably kissed lots of women on his many voyages. She did not want to be one of a crowd. She shook her head. "No, I'm not particularly tired."

"Then come."

"It's rather late. I think I'll go to my cabin. But thanks all the same." She smiled and stood up.

He walked with her to the top of the main stairway where she paused. "Perhaps we shall meet on Bucare some time," she said, giving him a friendly wave.

"Perhaps," he replied, coolly. "Who knows!"

As Karen went down the stairway and walked along the corridor to her cabin, she felt a sense of loss. It was a pity, she thought, that their paths had crossed in such an awkward way. Whatever the reason for his diffidence in discussing *Tabara* she was not likely to find out until much later.

As she lay in her bunk she found it impossible to concentrate on *Hiawatha.* Again and again her thoughts reverted to the romantic moments she had shared with Michael. But after a while she made a determined effort to push him from her mind and used her imagination to conjure up the island of Bucare.

She fell asleep picturing herself in a flowered bikini running along a sun-drenched beach with the surf of the blue sea breaking over the golden sand. She would discover later that the sand on Bucare was not gold, but silver, and that the water was aquamarine and so crystal clear that one could see the sea bed as far out as the coral reef at the edge of the lagoon.

3

IT was just beginning to get light, and it must have been the slowing down of the ship's engines that alerted Karen out of her sleep.

She looked out of her porthole to see dark rock shapes looming out of a grey-green mist as if they would touch the ship they were so close. But gradually, as her eyes became accustomed to the dim light, she could distinguish the dark shapes more easily and estimate the distance between them and the ship. They loomed for several minutes then receded and passed. There was an eerie quiet. What had happened to the ship's engines, for heaven's sake?

She dressed hurriedly, putting on slacks and her white woollen cardigan, then crept out of her cabin and went up on deck.

The *Camello* was travelling so slowly now as to seem almost at a standstill, and over the whole proceeding was a hushed expectancy with a remote pulsing somewhere in the bowels of the ship. Karen felt as if she was moving in a dream.

The indistinct shapes of the few silent passengers at the rail were like ghosts. She moved across to stand beside a tall shadowy figure who was obviously watching the ship's progress. "What's happening?" she whispered, almost afraid to speak. "Where are we?"

To her astonishment she realised it was Michael, though he showed no surprise at her presence.

"We are passing through The Dragon's Mouth," he answered. "The narrow channel that separates Trinidad from Venezuela."

Karen nodded and looked across the sea between the dark rocks to where a halo of pale green light now slowly illuminated the sky and began to streak it with rose and gold through the thick veil of morning mist.

Gradually the dark shapes receded altogether and there was a quickening tempo to the pulse of the engines. They had come through The Dragon's Mouth safely and the ship was now steadily making its way towards Port of Spain, the capital of Trinidad.

One by one the passengers began to converse in normal tones. Karen wandered towards the prow hoping that Michael might follow her, but he was watching the sea and looking up at the sky as if to question the weather. She was about to approach him again when all at once he turned and strode purposefully towards the main lounge. Disappointed, she stayed where she was a while longer before descending the companionway and making her way to the dining room.

A few minutes after she had given her order for a solitary light breakfast, Frances came through the swing doors and sat down beside her.

"Isn't Giles coming in for breakfast?" asked Karen.

Frances shrugged. "He's looking for Michael, who seems to have vanished. He might at least have had the decency to say goodbye." She seemed put out. "Oh well, if he wants to sneak off like that he's welcome," she added, then looked sharply at Karen. "I hope *you* haven't frightened him off."

When Karen did not reply, Frances laughed then tossed her head, suddenly regaining her good humour.

Giles appeared shortly afterwards. He sat down at the table and attacked his breakfast with gusto.

"Did you find Michael?" asked Frances.

Giles nodded. "He was talking to the Captain on the bridge. He requested me to extend his farewells to you both."

"Why couldn't he have done it in person?" Frances was piqued.

"Don't take offence, Fran," said Giles. "You know very well he'll want to take advantage of going across on one of the lighters."

Frances shrugged. "And that, I suppose, is the last we shall hear of Michael for months and months."

Karen changed the subject, it seemed the best thing to do. "How soon do you imagine we shall be able to disembark when once we dock?"

"The ship won't be docking for some time," replied Giles, consulting his watch. "But we usually get away about nine-thirty to ten. They have to get the bonded cargo ashore first." He paused to listen. "Sounds as if the engines have stopped. Come on, you two. Let's go up on deck and watch them drop anchor."

As they followed Giles up the stairway, Karen said, "I hope whoever is coming to meet me will have the patience to wait."

"Of course they will, you dolt." Frances gave her a withering glance.

As Giles held the door open for them to step out on deck he winked at Karen. Her discomfiture vanished. She liked Giles. He was so dependable . . . like a tree, she thought, remembering with amusement that he was a forestry officer.

They stood at the rail, looking down, watching a small craft being loaded with cargo, and when it was ready to depart they were surprised to see Michael call down to the skipper, then swiftly climb down the ship's side and jump into the loaded boat. A shout from a crew member above and his luggage was lowered on a rope. Michael looked up and waved to the crew member then set about stowing his possessions, and almost immediately the lighter moved off. Surely he hadn't cleared with Immigration so quickly!

The last Karen saw of him was the back of his blond tousled head as the lighter chugged away towards the docks. She watched it until it moved out of range then turned away. She felt no urgency now. She would go down to her cabin and check on her packing.

As she was making a final check that she had forgotten nothing the loudspeaker summoned the passengers to the main lounge.

Eventually, with formalitites completed, Karen, Frances and Giles, in company with others, were travelling across the water in the tender which would subsequently return to the ship to ferry the remainder of the passengers. It was only then, as they were travelling across the sea in the open boat, that Karen was able to put Michael out of her thoughts and concentrate on the adventure before her.

Standing on the dockside at last, she idly watched the stevedors and the colourfully dressed men and women who smiled and joked with one another. There was a kind of indolent sensuality in the way they moved their bodies. Their speech was musical and had a certain pleasing rhythm to it. She was astonished when she realised that it was a dialect English they spoke and that she could understand most of what they said.

She put down her case and almost immediately they were approached by a broad-shouldered bronzed man with a close haircut. He looked from Karen to Frances and back again. "Miss Warde?" he questioned, eyebrows raised.

"That's me," said Karen, relieved. "Are you Mr. Grant?"

"The very same," he replied, with a smile that somewhat disarmed her. "Laura Hammond is my mother. My father was her first husband." The statement was made automatically. He looked down at Karen's modest suitcase and enquired, "Is this all the luggage you have?"

She nodded. "It isn't much," she said, almost apologetically, "but I shall only be here for about three months." She turned to Frances and Giles. "I hate saying goodbye to you both."

"Don't worry," replied Frances. "We'll meet up again soon . . . I'm sure we shall. We know where you're staying."

Karen nodded and followed Warren

to the waiting cab. The windows were already down and she waved as they drew away from the dockside.

"Friends of the voyage?" Warren's voice had a lazy Southern accent.

"Yes," replied Karen. "They live in Port-of-Spain." She was aware that Warren Grant was appraising her. She wondered if he had expected someone different — perhaps older and more efficient-looking. However, he talked to her freely enough, telling her that it would take them about five minutes to reach the quayside where he had moored the pirogue.

"Forgive my ignorance," said Karen, "but what is a pirogue?"

"Let me see now . . . let's say that historically it was a hollowed out tree trunk used as a heavy canoe, but nowadays is a somewhat loose term for a cross between a barge and a large rowing boat. It has a deep draught and an inboard engine which is driven from a small forward cabin. How's that?"

Karen smiled. "Now I know what to expect."

"It's a very convenient craft. We collect our provisions from the mainland in it. It manoeuvres the swamps well, too."

"Swamps?"

"Yes, swamps. Not extensive though, and none in Bucare. Crab hunting in the Caroni swamps is a fine sport for the youngsters of Trinidad. Have you never heard of the legendary Scarlet Ibis that nests in the swamps of Trinidad?"

"I'm afraid not."

Warren grinned. "Then we shall have to complete your education."

She glanced at him as opportunity arose, and noted that his closely cropped hair was brown and curly. There was more than a suggestion of hard strength about him.

"Are there shops on Bucare?"

"A few small local shops. A coke bar, a hops bread shop, a chandler and a haberdashery — very limited, I'm afraid."

Karen was disappointed. She speculated on whether to ask what hops bread was, but let it pass. She discovered later that it was a large, very light, crusty type of French white bread roll.

"Not even a post office?" she pursued.

"No. There never has been one of Bucare."

"What happens about letters?"

"We collect our mail from the Trinidad head Post Office."

The cab driver negotiated his way through the ever increasing volume of traffic. Karen had never seen so many huge American cars being used as cabs. Horns blared, sometimes conversationally and sometimes argumentatively; it was obvious that most of the drivers were known to each other.

Warren Grant spoke. "We are almost at the quayside. Hold on."

The cab driver swung round in a wide arc and pulled up fast within inches of the sea wall. Warren paid him off and helped Karen out of the cab, taking personal charge of her luggage.

She followed him to some stone steps. He turned to hold her arm so that she could descend with safety to where the water slapped unpredictably. He tossed her things into the pirogue and made sure that she stepped carefully over the side and into the well of the boat which was exactly as Warren had described it. He indicated the bench seat in the forward cabin and set her luggage down on the wooden floor beside her.

"Here we go, then," he said, turning on the ignition.

The slow and cumbersome craft chugged away from the quayside and began the journey across to Bucare on a calm sea.

There was a strong smell of fish coming from the stern, and looking down Karen saw a basket of red snappers and two larger fish which she subsequently identified as Kingfish. Beside these varieties was a heap of very large shrimp laid out on a piece of sacking. They were still in their transparent uncooked state, yet nevertheless she eyed them with anticipation.

She wandered outside the cabin and looked across to the rapidly disappearing mainland where she could see hazy blue triple peaks in the far distance. Further along the coast of Trinidad she could see a fringe of palm trees. They appeared to stretch for miles, and a longing to go to such a place grew more and more as the distance widened. Would it be the same on Bucare, she wondered. She also wondered how soon it would be before she could visit Trinidad again. Port-of-Spain would be an exciting place to explore, and perhaps she could visit Frances and Giles.

They had been progressing steadily when Karen at last gave up gazing at Trinidad and looked out to sea. There were several small craft within sight, but it was a larger one on the horizon that held her interest. It had billowing scarlet sails and was sailing well before the wind. She gaped at its beauty and speed.

"Just look at that yacht," she called to Warren. "Isn't it magnificent!"

"It's a ketch, not a yacht," Warren called back, apparently uninterested.

Undismayed, Karen stood leaning over the side to watch the vessel as it gradually came nearer, passing across their bows at an even greater speed. Karen shielded her eyes with her hand trying to get a better view. She could just make out two figures standing at the rail – a man and a woman. Unable to resist an impulse, she waved, but only the girl returned her gesture. "I wonder who they are," she said aloud.

Warren turned his head to look at Karen, but he never answered her question. He turned his attention to the wheel.

Karen continued to watch the scarlet sails until she saw the ketch disappear round a small headland. She had been so intent on watching the craft she had not realised that the pirogue was close to the shore of a small island.

"Welcome to Bucare," said Warren.

Karen was unprepared for what she saw. The verdant landscape rose steadily in undulating sweeps to the summit, where a riot of flowering trees crowned the island like a garland. She held her breath, letting it out as a sigh. "How beautiful!"

Warren laughed. "Do you mean the island or the flowering trees?"

"All of it. It's heavenly."

"It's okay, I guess. But like everywhere in this world, it has its drawbacks at times."

"That's hard to believe."

Warren cut the engine as the momentum carried them towards a low gabled boathouse. As they coasted into it the light was dim after the brightness of the sea where the aquamarine water was so clear Karen could see the silver sand and pebbles beneath it quite clearly.

Warren looped a rope over a handrail and offered his hand to Karen so that she could mount some steps onto a wooden platform which ran round three sides of the boathouse. She could smell the wood; it held the tang of the sea, a delicious odour.

She waited expectantly listening to the water as it licked the sides of the boathouse. Warren passed up her case and she attempted to lift it.

"Leave it," he ordered. "I'll bring it up later when I collect this other stuff. Come. My mother will be waiting."

Karen followed him through a door and saw that on the outside of the boathouse was a stairway that ran upwards to another door. There must be a room over the boathouse.

Warren went ahead and Karen made an effort to keep up with him, but the sun was hot and she was becoming acutely aware of the humidity. Her sensitive skin prickled and moistened.

They walked between hibiscus hedges where a humming-bird was darting from blossom to blossom, its violet and green iridescent body flashing in the sun as its wings vibrated impossibly fast.

They emerged onto a freshly mown lawn of coarse grass. Karen was vaguely aware of her pounding heart as she strove to match Warren's pace but was uncertain as to its cause. She felt nervous at meeting her new employer. Old Mr. Arnold had been her only experience of employers and she wanted to make a good impression.

They were now approaching a wide verandah framed by kentia palms about one metre high, and as Karen stepped up into the shade onto a black marble floor a cold shiver ran down her spine at the contrast in temperature.

They passed through a wide sliding glass panel into an air-conditioned drawing-room, positively chilly, where Mrs. Laura Hammond awaited them.

Warren said briefly. "I'll fetch Miss Warde's luggage and leave it in the hall."

Laura Hammond rose from her chair and walked towards Karen, extending a limp hand in greeting. She was nothing like Karen had imagined, and realised at once that the limp handshake indicated a lack of enthusiasm for her visitor.

Laura Hammond radiated an almost masculine presence, and yet was so tiny she could not have been taller than about four feet eight or nine. She was dainty and dressed with impeccable taste. But it was when she smiled that there was a hint of the unshakable confidence that lay behind it. In the future, Karen would meet that implacable will head on, but at that moment she was anxious to make a good impression.

"So you are here. I trust you had a good journey." Her voice, like Warren's, had the soft southern intonation.

Karen nodded. For an instant her own voice had failed her.

"I hope you'll settle in comfortably with us whilst you are working here, Miss Warde." Her head tipped to one side as she regarded Karen's appearance without letting her eyes stray down and up more than once.

At a loss for something to say, Karen looked out of the window and, seeing the garden, remarked, "I have never seen such a beautiful island." She paused, then added, "It's like something one dreams about."

Laura Hammond merely smiled and walked across to the writing table on the far wall. She picked up a small brass hand-bell and rang it. "I'll get Theresa to show you to your room."

Theresa, apparently, was the maid, and when she appeared Karen took an instant liking to her. Though her expression was at that moment serious, Karen sensed that it would not be long before she smiled. It was a face that was more used to smiles than tears.

Theresa was a tall, rangy coloured girl, slow and deliberate in all her actions. Even her speech was slow and deliberate. But why was she wearing shoes that were so heavy and obviously a size or two too big?

"You rang, Mistress Hammond?" Theresa's dark eyes opened wide as she stood waiting and casting curious sideways glances at Karen.

"Yes, Theresa. Will you take Miss Warde up to the room we have made ready for her."

"Yessum. Dudley already done take up she luddage, and I done spray she press." Karen was intrigued by her way of speaking.

"Good girl, Theresa. Take Miss Warde up then, and be sure you show her where everything is."

"Yessum."

Karen followed Theresa along the passage, through the hall and up the staircase, noting that not only had she come to a beautiful island, she had come to a beautiful house. It was spacious and light, and the colour harmony of the furnishings was so subtle as to be hardly noticeable.

They reached the landing and Theresa opened a door on the right. Karen followed her into a pleasant room.

Theresa went across to a window the whole width of the room. She drew aside long lace drapes to reveal a breathtaking view of the sea, then turned to Karen, coyly cupping one of her ungainly hands to her mouth, and giggled. "Miss Karen, you'm have to watch out. That hair! She alive with fire."

Karen laughed. Theresa was a gem. At least there would be one kindred spirit in the house.

Still giggling, Theresa walked to the door. "The bathroom it through there." She pointed to a door opposite the window. "Evenin' meal six-thirty p.m. Mistress Hammond like people punctual."

"I'll remember, Theresa. Thank you."

The maid went off, talking to herself, her voice growing fainter as she descended the stairs.

Karen surveyed her room. The lace drapes that Theresa had pulled open revealed doors to a balcony. Karen attempted to open them but they appeared to be stuck. Later, she decided, she would ask Warren to open them. It would be more comfortable to be able to open the room to the night air. Then she noticed that running round the entire room at ceiling level were white painted wooden louvres, permanently open. These were obviously meant to be adequate ventilation.

The bed had brass rails and knobs,

and a canopy with net drapes completely surrounded it, suspended from a frame at ceiling level. Karen concluded that there must be mosquitoes to contend with.

Along the wall to the right of the bed was a built-in wardrobe which contained some shelves. The interior smelled deliciously clean with an odour partly disinfectant and partly some scent unknown to her. She discovered later that it was couscous grass.

She opened her case and hung her meagre wardrobe on some of the numerous hangers provided. Her few garments looked quite lost, so she spaced them widely. She would hope to supplement them as opportunity arose. It would be fun to explore the shops in Trinidad. Perhaps Frances would come with her.

The bathroom which led off her bedroom was small but well appointed. There was no bath, just a shower unit, but it was adequate for her needs. She glanced at her watch. It was already six o'clock. She must hurry, but there was time to try out the shower.

Laura Hammond was still in the

drawing room when Karen made her entrance.

"Would you care for a sherry before supper, Miss Warde?"

Karen hesitated.

"You are not used to the habit?"

"It isn't that, Mrs. Hammond. It's just that it is already six-thirty and Theresa impressed upon me that you like people to be punctual for meals. I don't want to cause any delay."

Laura Hammond smiled. "I believe it more likely that Theresa herself likes to get supper over quickly, so that she can get away."

"Doesn't she live in, then?"

"Oh yes. But her time is her own after supper."

"I see." Karen smiled.

There was a rustle of a newspaper. Karen located it to an armchair in the corner by a window. A bright-eyed old lady was peering at her over gold-rimmed spectacles, her white curly hair ruffled about her face like a bonnet. "Have you seen my nephew?" she asked.

Karen looked at the old lady and then at Laura Hammond, puzzled by the sudden question.

Laura Hammond ignored the remark but stepped forward. "Let me introduce you to Aunt Hattie," she said, and raising her voice slightly, she continued, "Hattie, this is Miss Karen Warde. She has come to do some work for me. She will be staying with us for a time."

"What kind of work?"

"Oh, just making a list of some books."

"What books?" The old lady was not to be put off.

"Arthur's books, Hattie. The ones in the library."

"But they are Arthur's books. He doesn't like people rummaging about in his study." Hattie was getting agitated.

"Hattie, you know very well that Arthur isn't with us any more. He died. A year ago. You must understand."

"Well I don't. And where's the boy? He's gone too. Why? I don't even remember Arthur saying goodbye." She began to cry. Tears welled in her eyes and spilled down onto her newspaper.

Karen looked on helplessly. She had the strangest urge to comfort the old dear.

Laura Hammond handed Aunt Hattie a tissue from a box on the table beside her and the old lady dabbed at her eyes.

"Now, come along, Hattie. Supper is on the table." She helped her up and took hold of her arm, guiding her out of the drawing room. "This way, Miss Warde."

The dining room looked out on a flower garden which was accessible through a french window that led on to a paved patio. A rustic extension with a shingle roof housed garden furniture, and wired to posts were segments of bark on which a variety of orchids flourished.

"What do you think of my garden, Miss Warde?"

Karen turned quickly from her admiration of it. "I still cannot get over all I'm seeing. Everything is so lovely here. It makes me want to explore."

"You will have plenty of time for that. Warren will be glad to show you the island."

"Certainly. And with pleasure." He had entered unobserved and was sitting at the opposite end of the table to his mother.

As they settled, a fifth member of the family came in. He was a boy of fourteen or fifteen and took his place somewhat truculently beside Karen. No-one made any attempt to introduce him and he was more or less ignored.

When Karen first saw him come in, she got the feeling she had seen the boy somewhere before. But that is nonsense, she chided herself. How could I possibly?

Warren took up the conversation. "When are you starting work, Miss Warde? You have a formidable task before you."

"Whenever Mrs. Hammond wishes. This evening?"

"Good gracious no!" Laura Hammond shook her head. "Tomorrow morning is quite soon enough."

"I shall look forward to it," said Karen. "What time would be convenient?"

"My, you *are* keen," cut in Warren. "You'll think differently when you find out how hard it is working in this climate."

"But doesn't air-conditioning take care of that?"

"To a certain degree, I suppose." He frowned. "But it will take a you a while to get used to. I guess the best way is for you to discover for yourself what it's like."

It was a great relief to Karen that the meal was informal. The food was simple, but delicious. Grilled steak and baked jacked potatoes and a truly splendid salad incorporating all manner of ingredients hitherto unfamiliar to her.

At the end of the first course the silent boy asked to be excused. Laura Hammond merely nodded and he left hurriedly. His absence improved the atmosphere, but no-one referred to his abrupt departure. Karen wondered if he even had a name.

"That was Harvey," said Warren, as if divining her thoughts.

"Oh." What else could she say?

Another small brass hand-bell rested beside Laura Hammond's plate and she lifted it to summon the maid to clear the plates.

Theresa came in laboriously pushing an empty trolley. She collected the dishes and plates, clattering them together in a haphazard fashion, then pulled the trolley after her as if to use it had been a condition of her employment. More clattering sounds emanated from the kitchen, and *Oh, Lordy!* was repeated several times before the trolley reappeared.

On the trolley was a superbly garnished ice-cream pudding, and on Theresa's head was a narrow brimmed straw hat.

Karen felt a surge of merriment. She looked down studiously at her plate.

Theresa solemnly placed the dessert and serving plates before Laura Hammond then made a slow dignified exit to the kitchen.

Warren caught Karen's eyes. "Theresa always wears a hat to go to the refrigerator," he grinned. "If she doesn't put it on she is convinced she'll get a fever."

Karen made a valiant effort to stifle her amusement.

Even Laura Hammond smiled. "We've had Theresa for many years now," she said, indulgently.

After supper, Karen gratefully withdrew and went to her room. Although it was only seven o'clock darkness had come swiftly. She was very tired. It had been a long exciting day.

She sat on the stool at the dressing table which would be hers for the next few months and looked at her reflection without seeing herself clearly. She yawned. "I might as well go to bed," she sighed. Then remembering Theresa, said "*Oh, Lordy!*" and laughed softly as she undressed.

4

KAREN was comfortable and slept well. Her bedroom was not air-conditioned and she was glad of it, for the cool trade winds fanned her limbs as she lay beneath the filmy canopy, secure from mosquitoes.

Unaccustomed scents teased her as she tried to identify them, and as she lay back on her pillows she could see tall palm trees silhouetted in black against a velvet blue sky alight with stars like tiny flickering lamps, so very different from London. At this time of the year, particularly, the contrast was so great.

She thought about the bookshop that was now so far away, and visualised old Mr. Arnold as he sat at his roll-top desk regardless of the leaking and rattling of the ancient window frames. She could not help smiling affectionately for the kind way he had secured her a berth on the *Camello*.

The journey to Bucare seemed like a

dream now that it was over. She sighed as her thoughts lingered on that final evening with Michael Williamson and realised how disappointed she felt that she would probably never see him again. His remembered kiss still came to her lips and the strength of his arms was still with her as she relived those magic moments.

Why had he been so distant afterwards? And why did he not say goodbye? It would not have cost him much effort, surely. Was he afraid, perhaps, that she might have asked him to take her to Bucare since they were both bound for that small island? How had *he* travelled to Bucare, anyway?

She sighed and turned on her side as Warren Grant now came into focus. What was he really like? He had been pleasant enough on the trip across from Trinidad, but that was as far as her consciousness went. Tired out from the excitement of her crowded day, the last thing she remembered was the movement of dark shapes advancing and receding in the early morning mist of the Gulf of Paria as the ship manoeuvred its way slowly through The Dragon's Mouth.

The accompanying eerie silence was an experience she would never forget.

And now it was morning. Karen looked at her watch, but it had stopped. She had forgotten to wind it.

There was a knock on her door. It was Theresa, who had brought her a breakfast tray of orange juice, a steaming hot pot of coffee, toast and preserves. She set it on the table beside the bed.

"Mornin' Miss Karen. Mistress Hammond say you come into the library at eight o'clock."

"Good morning, Theresa." Karen sat up quickly and hugged her knees with happy anticipation at the new day. "What's the time now?"

"Seven o'clock. Plenty time."

"Thank you. Tell Mrs. Hammond that I'll be there." She took a sip of her orange juice. It tasted quite different from what she was used to. It must have been made from fresh oranges, prepared that very morning. The coffee, too, was fragrantly delicious, and so were the huge white rolls, as light as a feather, yet crusty, and just warmed through. These were probably the *hops* bread Warren mentioned.

By five minutes to eight she had showered and dressed ready to start work. She had put on a soft green sleeveless shift that she knew would be comfortable, then bunched her hair, tying it up off her neck with a scarf.

Feeling businesslike, she descended the stairs and made her way along a passage to where she thought the library might be. The door was open and through it she could see the books — all four thousand of them — waiting for her attention. Her spirits rose at the prospect of listing them all. All her life she had loved books.

She hesitated at the open door and tapped softly.

"Come." Laura Hammond was waiting over by a wide bay window, and as Karen walked into the room the air-conditioning rippled over her bare arms like cold water, making her shiver. Involuntarily she crossed her arms, using her hands to shield herself from the unexpected chill.

Laura Hammond gave a wry smile. "You'd better fetch a cardigan, Miss Warde."

"I didn't realise the air-conditioning could be so cold." She shivered again.

"It's because you aren't used to it yet. You'll be very glad of the lower temperature when you get going on your task."

"I'll be as quick as I can." She turned and ran upstairs to fetch her white woollen jacket and was down again almost immediately.

Laura Hammond indicated the book-shelves, tight with volumes from ceiling to floor on three walls. "It's quite a formidable prospect," she observed. "I hope you are equal to it."

"Mr. Arnold wouldn't have sent me if he'd had any doubts, Mrs. Hammond." Karen gave a friendly smile.

But Laura Hammond did not respond. Instead, she said, "Well, we shall have to see, shan't we!" She paused, looking about her. "I have to go across to Trinidad today." She consulted her watch. "Right now I want to give Theresa her instructions, but I shall be back to see how you are settling in before I leave for the mainland. Seat yourself at the desk and see if I have forgotten anything."

Karen glanced at the desk where pens and paper had been put in readiness.

"Now, if you'll excuse me," said Laura Hammond, then left the room.

Once again Karen glanced around the shelves at the splendid collection of books. Now that she was alone she could investigate.

She walked over to a set of leather-bound volumes and picked one out at random. It was written in French – an original Balzac – *Une Ténébreuse Affaire*. The work had been serialised in 1841, but this was his authorised edition, printed in 1842. And beside this were others – not all Balzac – but just as interesting. Karen replaced the book and sighed with satisfaction. She was really going to enjoy her task.

In the centre of the room was a heavy oak desk and it was standing on a Persian rug about eight by six metres. Beneath the Persian rug was a carpet in soft blues and browns, which covered the floor entirely. Solid-looking leather chairs and a ladder-trolley were placed near the bookcases.

Karen sat down in the swivel-chair and swung herself round, then ran her fingers over the honey-coloured embossed leather blotting pad which she was to find very useful. She could tuck a half-completed page into a corner of it – it just fitted.

She sat back and again let her eyes rove over the four thousand-odd books awaiting her attention. The challenge excited her. Even handling books was a tactile pleasure to her, an adventure in itself, for she would certainly discover many volumes she had never seen or read.

It was difficult to believe that such a comprehensive library should exist on such a small remote island in the Caribbean. Someone must have worked hard to establish the collection. It was even more difficult to believe that anyone should wish to dispose of it.

In comparison with libraries in various houses she had visited before, all that was missing was a fireplace, but of course, that would have been an absurd notion in such a hot climate.

On the left of the window wall was an oil painting of a hunting scene, and on the right a faded patch on the soft green emulsion that now showed faintly yellow. It was obvious that at some time previously a companion painting had hung there. Where was it now, Karen wondered. Gone to be cleaned, perhaps. She jumped suddenly, awkwardly. Laura Hammond was standing behind her chair.

"I'm sorry, Mrs. Hammond," she said, guiltily. "I didn't realise you had come back already."

"No doubt you were completely carried away in the contemplation of your gargantuan undertaking."

"Contemplating, yes, but not in the least daunting. I'm going to love the work. I can't help feeling that this collection was put together by someone who loved books."

Laura Hammond took a deep breath. "Yes, well, there it is. He is not here to enjoy it, now."

Karen waited.

"It was my husband, of course. He lived here for many years before I came. I was his second wife."

"Would that be Mr. Arthur Hammond?"

"Yes. He died a year ago." She turned away for a moment then became brisk. "Well, now, Miss Warde. I think I had better ask if there is anything more you need, or want to know, before you start." She raised her eyebrows.

"I don't think so. Everything seems very straightforward. But have you any *particular* instructions?"

"No. Except that I want every single volume listed. Not one must be missed."

"I will certainly make sure of that."

"Oh, there is just one thing. When you type the final list, will you make sure there's a free column on the right. For valuation purposes, you understand."

"Certainly. I'll do that." Karen glanced across to a side table. "I presume it is all right for me to use that typewriter."

"Of course." She put a finger to her forehead. "Oh yes . . . I knew there was something else. I'd like six copies of the final list. You'll find some carbons in the desk drawer, no doubt." She walked to the door. "Just one other thing. I don't think you should work more than four or five hours on your first day. This afternoon you should go out – have a look round. Warren will be here to accompany you."

Karen smiled. "I shan't need to worry him, Mrs. Hammond. But thank you, all the same."

"Oh, I almost forgot. Help yourself to some lunch. There is always something in the refrigerator. If you can't find what you want, ask Theresa. I'll see you at supper time."

Karen settled at her desk and concentrated on ruling up pages of foolscap which would assist her in categorising. Most of the volumes were grouped, but she might well find that her training would lead her to catalogue differently. She would have to see.

So happily did she slip into her work that when a knock came on the door and Theresa entered, bearing a small round tray with a tall cool drink of lime juice she could hardly believe that half the morning had gone already.

As Theresa placed the tray on a side table Karen turned to her with a smile. But Theresa placed a finger to her lips. She had obviously been given instructions not to disturb.

Karen worked on steadily until she began to feel hungry, and on looking at her watch she saw that it was already one o'clock.

When she opened the library door

the house was so quiet that it seemed deserted, and as she made her way to the kitchen her footsteps reverberated across the uncanny silence of the hallway.

In the kitchen all was serene and cool. The light panelled wood had a golden glow from the bars of sunlight shining through the venetian blinds at the large windows. And as if the blinds were not enough, there was a wide ceiling fan, making doubly sure of controlled comfort.

She looked about her. A pot of coffee was showing a pilot light.

She opened the refrigerator and took out a box of salad.

"Is there any coffee going?" asked a voice from the doorway.

Karen looked up from helping herself to salad, surprised to see Warren Grant watching her. How long had he been standing there? She was disconcerted, embarrassed at helping herself to food in a strange house. She did not speak, but gathered her wits sufficiently to point to the coffee pot and its winking pilot light.

Warren Grant took down two cups and

saucers and moved towards the coffee pot to flick the switch.

"I thought you had taken your mother across to the mainland," said Karen.

"That was hours ago." He poured two cups of coffee and handed her one.

"Thank you," Karen replied, somewhat primly. Her full lips tightened a little and a tiny frown came and went. Disinclined for conversation with her mind still on books, Warren Grant's easy familiarity made her uneasy. He was, as yet, an unknown personality to her, and it occurred to her to wonder if the two of them were alone in the house. Where was Theresa?

Karen continued helping herself to salad, though she took very little. She turned to Warren with a questioning look before replacing the lid, holding the box towards him. He took it from her and placed it onto the counter between them. He then opened the refrigerator and took out a bowl of potato salad and placed it within reach.

Karen had no option to mount a stool and sit at the counter.

Warren pushed her cup of coffee

towards her and sat beside her. She would have much preferred to find a tray and remove herself to the study, but Warren, apparently, took it for granted that they would eat together.

"How's the job going?" His enquiry appeared to be genuine interest.

"I have only just started on it."

"Perhaps you already regret taking it on."

"Of course I don't. I love books." Her reply was sharp.

"You aren't very friendly. Have I done anything to annoy you?"

"Of course not, Mr. Grant. But I didn't imagine being friendly was part of my contract. I've come here to catalogue four thousand books, and naturally it's a big responsibility."

Warren laughed. "My! You talk as if the cares of the world are on your shoulders."

Karen felt his eyes on her, willing her to smile at him and found herself relenting.

"You have a very nice smile," he said. "You should practice it more often."

Karen laughed.

Encouraged, Warren said, "How about calling me by my christian name? Mr. Grant is pretty stuffy."

Karen picked up her cup and saucer intending to help herself to a second coffee.

"Let me." Warren was on his feet immediately.

She thanked him, adding, "Could we forget about christian names for the time being, please? Somehow I don't think your mother would approve of our being too familiar so soon. Don't you agree?"

Warren shrugged. "As you please, Miss Warde, but as I said before, I was only trying to be friendly." He placed her second cup of coffee carefully beside her plate and strode off, leaving her alone and very uncomfortable. Now I've done it, she thought, but I don't care. I'm not sure I trust him, anyway. I don't want to be unsociable but I must get my bearings before I encourage friendship with Warren Grant. Everything is so strange. I'm not even sure that Mrs. Hammond approves of me. She scares me a bit. She was relieved to return to her books.

At three o'clock Karen left the library and found her way to the edge of the tiny harbour. The sun was hot, but because of the humidity it was not unpleasantly so, and a gentle breeze was blowing in from the sea.

Looking out over the water she saw the ketch with the scarlet sails again. It was riding at anchor about a hundred yards off shore.

Shading her eyes with her hand she could just make out the name on the prow. *Ibis.* Then behind her she heard laughing voices and, turning, saw Michael Williamson and a fair girl walk down to a dinghy at the water's edge. Karen's heart turned over, suddenly envious of the girl he was with.

She watched Michael pull the starter cord on the outboard motor and the two went skimming across the water. They appeared to be making for the *Ibis.*

Karen turned away and walked towards a couple of small shops. At least he didn't see me, she thought, feeling a rush of emotion and recognising it as disappointment. Oh well, she reasoned, a man like that is bound to have plenty of women friends. However much she tried not to, though, her mind swished in turmoil as she remembered the evening when he asked her if they might be friends. How he had sought her out on that last evening after having left her alone for the whole voyage. It had been a strange way to behave. And then, when he had kissed her . . . yes . . . that kiss had seemed so real . . . as if he had really meant it. She could not believe he was just being casual.

She had walked some distance beyond the two small shops when a hand touched her shoulder. She spun round to confront the very person she had been thinking about.

"Hello," he greeted her.

"Oh!" Karen gasped. "Just a moment ago you were in a dinghy, making your way out to sea."

"I was ferrying my passenger across. I thought I'd come back and have a word with you. You got here all right, I see."

"Yes." She could feel her colour rising. "I'm staying at *Tabara*," she added, lamely.

"So you told me. How's the job going?"

"It's rather too soon to ask that," she smiled. "I only started on it today."

He grinned. "You like books?"

Karen nodded. "I adore them . . . and the library at *Tabara* is such a beautiful room to work in."

"Yes, it is quite pleasant."

She looked at him in surprise. "You know it?"

"Yes. I know it well."

She waited for some enlightenment, but he said nothing more about the library. She was very tempted to ask him if he remembered the pictures; her curiosity about the faded empty space might have been satisfied, but she refrained.

"Don't let them work you too hard," he joked.

"Oh, they are being very kind. Mrs. Hammond decreed that I shouldn't work very long today. She told me to go for a walk." She paused, aware of the way he looked at her. "So that's what I'm doing," she added, lamely.

He lingered awhile. "I'll probably see you again, Karen. It's a very small island." Then with a cheery wave he strode back to the dinghy, started the outboard motor and skimmed across the water to the *Ibis*.

She watched him with mixed emotions. Standing at the rail was the girl she had seen him with earlier. She saw Michael climb aboard and wondered if he might turn to wave, but she was disappointed. Then she noticed that Warren Grant, also, was staring at the ketch, though his expression was not one of pleasure.

"Hi there!" Karen called lightly, in an effort to be friendly. "I hope you don't think I'm playing truant. Your mother suggested I finish work at three."

Warren sauntered towards her, his manner cool. "I'm not spying on you, Miss Warde." He frowned. Karen knew he was put out, and blamed herself.

Warren inclined his head in the direction of the *Ibis* and raised his eyebrows. Karen, for some obscure reason, felt compelled to offer an explanation for the encounter. "Michael Williamson was one of the passengers on the *Camello*," she said. "He was just passing the time of day."

"No doubt you told him all about the reason for your visit to *Tabara*."

"Why yes," she replied. "Is there any reason why I shouldn't have?"

He did not reply immediately.

Karen hesitated then turned as if to go.

He caught her arm. "I'm sorry. I didn't mean to sound churlish, but there's something I think you ought to know." He paused. "My mother won't be pleased if you get too friendly with Mike Williamson. So far as she is concerned he is *personna non grata* in our household."

Karen's eyes opened wide with incredulity. "Why ever?" I don't believe it, she thought. "He seems a perfectly reasonable person to me."

"I'm warning you. That's all."

Karen turned her back on him. She was furious. She wanted to defend Michael against such a preposterous pronouncement . . . and yet what did she really know about Michael? She walked away, fuming. I'm hanged if I'm going to be dictated to as to what friends I make, she determined, and hurried on.

Warren caught up with her, saying that he would come with her.

"I'd rather you didn't," she retorted.

"I'm not ready to go back yet." She hesitated then changed her direction. "That store over there looks interesting."

"I'll wait for you."

"Please don't. I want to have a browse," she said. "I might find something interesting to take back as a souvenir."

"I should very much doubt it. However, I don't suppose you'll take my word for it."

Karen laughed. "No. You can certainly be sure of that." She went on ahead, hoping to shake him off. But still he followed her. Going for a walk wasn't going to be much fun if Warren Grant was looking over her shoulder the whole time. She turned and said, "What do I have to do to persuade you not to trail after me? I have asked you politely. I can find my way back to *Tabara* quite easily."

Warren regarded her fixedly. "I guess I know when I'm not wanted," he said, frowning and walking away.

Karen breathed a sigh of relief and entered a tiny crowded shop to find a complete jumble of dusty artifacts which were mostly fishing tackle and odds and ends connected with boating. There were one or two brightly coloured garments on hangers, high up, but they had obviously been there for years and were faded and grubby with age.

She peered about in the dim interior for anything at all she might find of interest, and had almost given up hope when she spotted a large clam shell. It, too, had obviously lain there for a very long time, but it intrigued her. She had an urge to own it, to scrub it clean and polish it. She felt she had never seen such a beautifully formed object and tried to lift it, only to discover that it was very heavy. She wondered how it would be possible to get it back to *Tabara*.

She looked up to see a smiling brown face watching her, and she smiled back. The man looked more like a fisherman than a storekeeper.

"How much?" She rocked the shell back and forth, testing its manoeuvrability and speculating whether she could possibly carry it.

The fisherman shook his head. "It heavy, heavy," he replied.

"But how much do you want for it?"

"I give it to you. That ol' clam been there ten year. What you want he for?"

"It's so beautiful. But I *must* pay for it."

"No, no. You buy candle. I give you shell. Okay?"

"Done." Karen searched among the artifacts for candles, but could see none."

"Not there," said the storekeeper. "Here." He disappeared behind a tangle of netting and canvas sacks to reappear holding a box of coloured candles. Karen had no idea what she could do with them, but she felt the occasion demanded some enthusiasm.

At the back of the store a lace curtain moved a child's voice called, "Winston? What you doin'? You done promise take me fishin'."

"You wait, Miss Impatient. The customer come first."

Karen looked towards the dark corner, but all she could see was a small pair of legs clad in faded blue jeans. The face was hidden behind the lace curtain.

"Come out of there, Tracy. Come and meet the lady come to stay at the big house along the shore."

There was a coaxing moment before the child emerged from the shadows. Short plaits tied with red ribbon bows stuck out at right-angles from her head, but the eyes were large and brown and sparkling.

Karen smiled and said, "Hello, Tracy."

"Tracy not my real name. Winston call me that because I always runnin' down the trace."

"Trace?"

"Path to the sea," interposed Winston. "Path to anywhere. Tracy, she run away all the time."

"What is your proper name?"

"Ursula." She paused. "On account of I went to the Convent school."

"There's a school on Bucare?"

Tracy shook her head. "Trinidad. I don't go no more."

"No need," commented Winston.

Karen did not know quite what observation to make to such a statement. The girl was obviously no older than eight or nine. "I must admit that I like the name Tracy better than Ursula," she offered. "May I call you that?"

"If you like." She gave a wide grin,

displaying her perfect teeth.

Karen now gave her attention to her purchase. The box of candles had been placed on the wooden counter. "How much do I owe you, Winston?" It seemed natural to call him that.

"Two dollar."

"Will you keep them for me? I didn't bring any money with me today. I'll need to go back for some."

"No matter. Tracy, pick up the clam shell for the lady."

"No. It's far too heavy for Tracy. Leave it and I'll take the candles first, then come back for the shell when I bring the money."

Karen picked up the box of candles and Tracy followed her out of the store. It appeared that Tracy intended to accompany her.

"This way," indicated Tracy. "I show you the way back along the water." She ran ahead, eager to demonstrate her knowledge and obviously delighted at making a new acquaintance. Now and then she gave a little skip and ran back to urge Karen on.

Karen found walking on the hot sand

was hard going, and every now and then she had to stop and empty her shoes.

"Take they off," advised Tracy.

Karen made the attempt. "I can't. The sand burns my feet."

Tracy laughed and looked down at her own bare brown feet, then laughed gleefully and ran down to the water's edge. "Come," she called, wading into the water, and Karen had little choice but to take off her shoes and follow Tracy's lead.

The water was warm and seductive; it was all she could not to toss away her shoes and swim towards the coral reef. Instead, she waded out a little further and stood looking at the island.

To her right were tall coconut palms, and on the ground beneath them were creeping plants, pale bright green with rounded leaves. It was amazing how green they were when the sand was so dry. Stray coconuts lay where they had fallen, and some had lain long enough to sink into the sand and germinate, a single sturdy shoot that reached up into the sun like an unclenching green fist. The smell and sound of the sea, the sand and vegetation and the warm breeze roused her senses as never before.

She looked ahead to where Tracy was doing a balancing act along a recumbent coconut palm that had grown too close to the water and was now washed backwards and forwards with the waves. Its roots had long given up the struggle for survival. Tracy, with her arms outstretched to help her maintain her balance, looked amusing with her angled matching plaits.

Karen paddled on. How much further was it?

At last, when she had reached the fallen tree and made her way round it, she could see that there was a small bay ahead and there, also, was the gabled boathouse. *Tabara* reached tall behind a high hibiscus hedge.

Tracy again ran on ahead and disappeared completely. Karen made her way up to the house and went upstairs to her room to get some cash. When she came down again she was surprised to hear voices coming from the kitchen.

Peeping in she saw Tracy sitting up on the counter as if she owned the place. Theresa was opening a cookie jar and they seemed unaware of her until she walked in.

"So you two know each other!"

There was a burst of merry laughter from both.

"What's the joke?" Karen found herself laughing with them.

"She my baby," said Theresa.

Tracy grinned and swung her legs.

Karen looked at Theresa with astonishment and Tracy helped herself to another cookie.

"Then Winston . . . he's Tracy's father?"

"That so, Miss Karen. He fisherman. Me cook. Tracy here . . . " She gave her daughter a poke in the ribs and concluded, "She mischief," then smiled indulgently.

Tracy jumped down from her perch and said, "Ready?"

Karen nodded. "But I'm not struggling along the beach again. We'll go by the path — trace."

"Okay," said Tracy, dancing on one foot and then the other.

They got as far as the first corner when Warren appeared. He was carrying the clam shell as if it weighed hardly anything.

Karen, unsure of her appreciation for his help, waited for him to explain.

"Winston asked me to deliver it."

"But it's so heavy to carry all that way," said Karen. "Thanks, anyway." She paused. "I'll go along and pay him now." She looked around for Tracy. It would be convenient to let her have the money – but she had disappeared again.

Warren grinned. "It has been taken care of. I paid Winston the two dollars for the candles but I'll make you a present of them."

Karen laughed. "Thanks. Actually, I didn't bargain on buying candles. It was only the clam shell I wanted."

"Well, now that you have the candles, what are you going to do with them?"

"I can't imagine. Unless someone is due for a birthday soon." She opened the box and inspected the candles. "They look a bit bent to me," she said.

"It's the way they do business here." He moved his shoulders in explanation. "He has probably had those damn candles in store for years. He did something for you so you buy candles. Got it?"

"Quaint, but rather nice."

"What are you going to do with the shell, now that you own it?"

"Scrub and polish it."

"And then . . . ?"

"I haven't thought that far."

Warren continued to carry the shell and Karen walked beside him. When they reached *Tabara*, he said, "Where shall I put it?"

"Better leave it outside by the boathouse, I think. I won't take it into the house until it's clean."

He placed the shell on the bottom step of the wooden stairs leading to the upper floor of the boathouse. "Now that's done," he said, "I have a suggestion to put to you."

Karen looked at him, wondering what was coming.

"How about visiting the Caroni swamps with me?"

"The swamps?" For a moment she thought she had misheard.

"Yes. Caroni swamps. Over on Trinidad. It's where the scarlet ibis nest. But we shall have to go just before dusk to be sure of seeing them at their best."

"It sounds exciting. I've never heard of them before. I thought you meant the ketch with the scarlet sails for a moment. That's named *The Ibis*."

Warren's brow clouded. "No," he said, "not that."

There was a pause until Karen asked, "When were you thinking of going?"

"Tomorrow, perhaps, if that would suit you."

"Yes, of course – but I'll have to get permission from your mother."

"I think it highly unlikely that she will raise any objection, provided I am with you."

"Then I'll look forward to it," said Karen. "Shall I need to wear anything special?"

"No. Come as you are. But I do suggest you bring a warm jacket."

"What about mosquitoes?"

"Shouldn't be troublesome. It's sea water, remember."

Karen nodded. The prospect of visiting an unknown swamp at dusk sounded rather creepy and she was not sure whether she wanted to be alone in a boat at night with Warren. However, she put it out of her mind for the time being. Tomorrow evening was a long way off – almost anything might happen between now and then.

5

THE following morning Karen stood at her bedroom window contemplating the new day. The tip of the sun was casting shafts of golden light across the sea. The orb was rising as she watched, higher and higher it came, soon to drench the whole island in heat.

The temptation to go for an early morning swim was too great to resist.

She emerged from the house into a perfect sun-drenched tropical morning. Warm enough to be cool, yet not too cool. It was perfect. The air was soft it was almost touchable — like swansdown.

Her coffee-coloured one-piece bathing suit set off her trim figure as she ran lightly between the high hibiscus hedges down towards the boathouse. At the foot of the steps she listened. Someone was there before her!

She waited a few seconds and the door at the top of the steps opened. It was Harvey. He looked surprised, then reddened. As he came down Karen could see that he was carrying flippers.

"There are plenty more," he said, pointing upwards.

Karen smiled. "I've never worn flippers. What are they like?"

"They make a lot of difference. Try them." He ran back up the steps, apparently pleased to help her.

When he came down again he handed her a pair of flippers and when they reached the water's edge she put them on and stood up, indulging in an exaggerated walk for Harvey's amusement, then turned to find him grinning.

"Will you show me what to do?" she asked.

"There's nothing to do. Come on." He plunged into the water and swam out to where it was deeper. Karen watched him, and having demonstrated his own prowess she did her best to emulate him. They were so engrossed they did not see the ketch with the scarlet sails bearing down on them.

Harvey saw it first, but paid no attention until he suddenly caught sight of Michael at the helm. He flung up his arms with a cry of greeting. "Mike! When did you get back? It's real good to see you." He swam to the ketch and climbed on board where the two began a back-slapping exchange whilst Karen looked on, bobbing up and down in the water like a seal.

"You two know each other, I see," she called up.

"*Know each other!*" echoed Harvey. "We are *brothers.*"

Karen was non-plussed. "You *mean* it?"

"Of course. But Mike has been away for a long time."

"Idiot," returned Michael. "It has only been three months. A man needs a change now and again."

"Anyway," said Harvey, "how come you two know each other?"

"We met on the ship coming over," said Michael.

Karen swam to the side of the ketch and Michael reached down to her. "Come aboard," he smiled, taking her hand and pulling her up on deck.

"How was the trip to Iceland?" Harvey wanted to know.

"Fascinating, interesting, satisfying, but very cold."

"Three months was quite enough, then?"

"It was indeed. It's good to be back."

"Have we got time for a quick run round the point before breakfast, Mike?" Harvey was already tugging at the spinnaker guy rope.

"I don't see why not," replied Michael. "In fact, I was going to suggest it." He turned to Karen. "I hope you'll come with us."

"I don't think I ought to. I have to be seated at the breakfast table by 8.30 a.m."

"We can easily get back by then," cut in Harvey. "You tell her, Mike."

Michael nodded. "We have done it before. I promise to get you back here by eight o'clock if you'll change your mind."

"Come on, Karen, do. Mike always keeps promises," urged Harvey.

She smiled. "You've both talked me into it," she said. "But don't forget, I'm on my best behaviour at the moment. I don't want Mrs. Hammond to scold me."

"Righto, then," said Michael. "Off we go. Harve. You take the helm and I'll deal with the sails."

Karen felt a surge of excitement as they turned into the wind and the sails billowed. The pure silence of sailing was intoxicating. The only sounds were the water lapping the hull and the occasional flick of canvas as they cut through the slight swell. Karen held on to the mizzen mast and set her face against the breeze and inhaled the smell of the sea. It was sheer heaven.

Michael came to stand by her when he had checked with Harvey at the wheel. "What do you think of the *Ibis*?"

"I think she's elegant. How long have you owned her?"

"About two years. She belonged to my stepfather, Arthur Hammond. He made me a present of her when she got just a bit too boisterous for him to handle. After he retired."

"Who kept her in such good trim whilst you were away?"

"Rosemary."

"That would be the girl I saw you with yesterday?"

"That's right."

Karen felt a twinge of jealousy. Who was Rosemary?

Michael walked to the side of the boat and took a rope in his hand. "Hove to leeward, Harve," he called over his shoulder as he fastened the rope to a cleat. Then turning back to Karen, he said, "She's not fast, but she's lively."

After a minute or two Karen said, "There's something that puzzles me. Why does Harvey live at *Tabara* but not you? Being brothers, I mean."

"Harvey and I are Arthur Hammond's stepsons. Our mother was Arthur's first wife who, like Laura, had been married before. *Her* first husband's name was Grant, Warren's father. Is everything clear to you, now?" He smiled down at her.

Karen nodded, a tiny crease appearing between her brows. "It's rather complicated, but I think I've got it. Your mother was married before, and her name then was Williamson."

"Correct. Any more questions?"

She smiled and shook her head. She hoped that she had not appeared over-inquisitive and left Michael with the impression that she was prying, or that some explanation was due.

He was looking at her again. "Would you like me to show you over?"

Her frown disappeared. "I'd love it." She looked about her. She could see that the *Ibis* was a two-masted ketch, the mizzen mast rising to about two thirds the height of the main mast. Michael explained that as the mizzen was fairly large, the mainsail was correspondingly reduced.

"Is this a racing boat?" Karen wanted to know.

Michael shook his head. "No. She's not particularly efficient for sailing against the wind – particularly more than a force four."

Karen looked blank and Michael laughed. "A fairly stiff breeze," he elucidated.

Michael again called to Harvey. "Keep the wheel steady. I'll take over when we come to the headland." He turned to Karen. "You had better put something over that wet suit. Here, have my reefer." And without waiting for an answer he took off his jacket and placed it around her shoulders and said, "This way."

He opened a light brown varnished hatchway and Karen could see that there were steps leading down into a cabin. Michael caught her arm. "Careful now, we don't want any calamities on your first visit."

"You had better go first then," she replied, standing back so that she could follow him.

At the bottom of the steps she looked round in amazement. The cabin was fitted out to a degree she would never had expected on board such a vessel, from outside appearances, that is. Everything was so neat, yet all the fittings were so functional. Michael showed her how cupboards and drawers were utilized to their full extent. There were fittings that even took care of crockery so that in rough weather cups, saucers and plates would be restrained against movement or breakage. A shower and lavatory unit was located at the rear, behind a small gallery, and a partition could be unfolded to divide the cabin up to make a bedroom and a sitting room.

Michael watched her face. "Sit down,

I'll make some coffee," he said, and went across to a small shelf where he plugged in a coffee pot.

"How can you run an electric appliance? Surely there is no electricity on board."

He smiled. "You must have seen gadgets plugged into cigar lighters in cars! This is on the same principle."

She watched him pull down a table-top which rested on a hinge fastened to the wall. The flap of it was large enough to extend halfway across the cabin so that it was accessible from the bench opposite.

As Karen continued to watch him she was puzzled as to the reason for Mrs. Hammond's antagonism towards Michael. He appeared to be such a straightforward person. Warren had scowled at the sight of him. She wished she knew why.

Harvey came down the steps. "She'll be okay for a bit. I smell coffee," he said, looking from one to the other.

Karen was momentarily disappointed at the interruption and Harvey, sensing it, drew back.

"Get the cups out, Bro'," said Michael, easily, his voice breaking the tension and making Harvey at ease. It was obvious to

Karen that Harvey was used to feeling he was in everybody's way.

The coffee was really hot and Karen sipped it gladly. How she wished that the interlude didn't have to end so soon.

As if he read her thoughts, Michael looked at his watch and said, "We must be getting back. It's half past seven already."

"My goodness!" Karen jumped to her feet.

Michael grinned. "It's not much use jumping back into the sea right now. You had better wait until we reach *Tabara.*"

She laughed as she handed Michael his reefer jacket. "Thanks," she said, "it was nice and warm."

"You had better keep it on until we get back."

Karen slipped the jacket round her shoulders then climbed the steps to the deck. As she sat on a coil of rope putting on her flippers again, Michael said, "How about coming sailing with me at the weekend?"

"That would be fun." She hesitated. "Would that be Saturday or Sunday?"

"Sunday. For the whole day."

"I should love to."

"Good. Watch out for me about seven o'clock."

"As early as that?"

He nodded. "I shall expect you to have breakfast with me. Harvey can make himself useful with the cooking."

"Harvey?" For some vague reason Karen had not expected the invitation to include Harvey. It made her feel selfish.

"Yes. He's quite a proficient cook."

"Is there anything you want me to bring?"

"Just yourself," he said, smiling down at her from his six foot height as she was poised to jump into the water. Harvey was already half way to shore.

Michael followed Karen's progress as she made her way slowly, doing the breast stroke. His thoughts turned to teaching her the crawl, but on reflection decided that no doubt Harvey would soon take care of that.

As Karen and Harvey walked up from the beach together, flippers in hand, Harvey said, "I suppose you're wondering about us. *And* my dear stepmother." He sounded bitter. "I *hate* her." He continued. "And so did Father when he found out what she was really like."

I want to ask questions, thought Karen, but I musn't tread on dangerous ground . . . perhaps just one, though. "Harvey, why isn't Michael welcome at *Tabara*? You might as well tell me."

He shrugged, then shook his head. "You've got it wrong. It's Mike who won't come *here*."

"Do you know why?"

He shook his head again. "No, I don't, and no-one will tell me. But I've gathered that it was something serious that happened." He paused. "All I know is that it was something to do with my father – when he was drowned, I mean."

"*Drowned?*" exclaimed Karen. "But I thought he died after a long illness!"

Harvey gave her a dark look. "I don't know where you got that idea from. I can assure you . . . he was drowned. I'm positive of that."

At the breakfast table Laura Hammond exhibited displeasure and there was an air of tension. Warren was absent and Harvey silent, as before.

Karen made no attempt at conversation. Aunt Hattie rattled on about nothing in particular, most of what she said being a repetition of what she had read in yesterday's newspaper. Now and again she gave Karen a knowing sideways smile, but did not address her directly. Perhaps she, too, sensed the tension.

Towards the end of the meal, Aunt Hattie left the room, and then Harvey departed, leaving Karen alone with Laura Hammond.

"Miss Warde, my son saw you boarding Michael Williamson's ketch early this morning. Tell me, have you known him long?"

"No, Mrs. Hammond. I don't know him very well at all, but he was a passenger on the ship I came over on. I was quite surprised to discover that he is Harvey's brother."

"Yes, that happens to be true. On the other hand, I think I should tell you that Michael Williamson is not someone you should associate with. You will oblige me by avoiding his company in future."

Karen gasped. "But . . . " An unexpected shaft of loyalty for Michael charged through her. For the moment she would ignore the comment, but more than that, she reacted strongly to having her freedom threatened. She stood up. "Mrs. Hammond, I wonder if I might ask you a question."

"What is it?"

"My hours of work. I should like to have some idea of what my free time will be."

"Of course. That is only reasonable. Well . . . I should imagine you will have had enough by about three o'clock each afternoon, since I notice you like to make an early start. No work on Saturdays or Sundays. How will that suit you?"

"Very well, thank you. I like to know where I stand. I want to get the cataloguing done as quickly as possible, but knowing exactly what you expect of me gives me a satisfactory guide-line so that I am free to do what I like in my spare time."

"Within limits, of course. It doesn't include running after Michael Williamson."

Karen swallowed hard. She had no intention of letting Laura Hammond intimidate her. She could feel rebellion rising, but she turned aside the unnecessary remark by telling her employer how much she appreciated being so close to the beach. "The water is marvellous, and so warm."

"Yes, it is, and the swimming is so safe. If you are interested there's snorkel equipment in the boathouse."

"Thanks. Harvey has already introduced me to flippers. I'm getting quite used to them. I'm hoping he'll give me a lesson or two in snorkelling." Then she changed the subject. "Do you know that your son has invited me to visit the Caroni swamp this evening?"

"Yes. He told me." She paused. "You may as well take the boy with you as well."

"You mean Harvey. Yes, that would be a good idea. I'm sure he'd be glad to come."

"How can you give an opinion on that, Miss Warde? You hardly know the boy."

Karen's colour mounted. Her good intentions were wasted. If she saw Harvey before they went she would ask him herself. "Excuse me, Mrs. Hammond. It's time for me to start work." Then without waiting to be dismissed she walked out of the room, her head held high. If Laura Hammond continued to bait her she would have to be doubly careful what she said in future. She opened the library door and closed it softly behind her. This is the room in the house where I feel happiest, she thought.

She sat down at the desk and pondered over the difficult conversation which had taken place at the breakfast table. What was it that made Laura Hammond take such a dislike to her? Surely it wasn't because her son was friendly towards her. Anyway, he was only being polite. He had more or less committed himself to showing her the local attractions when he ferried her over from Trinidad that first day. What was it he had said? "We shall have to complete your education, I can see." Yes, that was it. He was only following up his hospitable intentions.

Karen shook her head to rid her mind of extraneous thoughts and settled down to her work. Two hours later, Theresa knocked on the door and the frail figure of Aunt Hattie followed her in.

"I tell she you busy, Miss Karen, but she insist."

"That's all right, Theresa." Karen got up and fetched another chair, offering Aunt Hattie her own since it was more comfortable.

"Everybody gone to Trinidad," informed Theresa, conspiratorially, then withdrew.

Aunt Hattie was in an expansive mood and chattered away happily, sometimes to Karen and sometimes to herself. It was difficult to follow her flights of memory, but Karen eventually realised that it was Michael who was so much on the old lady's mind.

"It wasn't him at all, you know, dear. It was the other one," said Aunt Hattie, quite unexpectedly.

"Who do you mean?"

"I *told* you. It wasn't *my* boy, it was the other one."

"The other one?"

"Yes. The other one."

"Who are you speaking of?"

"I told you. I'm talking about Michael. He never said anything about it."

"About what, Aunt Hattie?" Karen was patient.

"You know about what. They all know. They think I don't, but I do."

"Know what, Aunt Hattie?"

At that moment Theresa came in with a tray of coffee and biscuits instead of the usual cold drink. Aunt Hattie took it upon herself to pour and handed Karen a cup as graciously as if she had been entertaining.

After a while, the old lady suddenly looked at Karen full in the face. "You're a nice kind girl, but you aren't one of the family, are you?" She looked round as if searching for something. "I must read yesterday's paper again," she continued. "There's sure to be something I've missed."

"How do you get the Trinidad papers so easily, Aunt Hattie?"

The old lady looked vague then got up from her seat. "Theresa gets them from Winston, of course. The fish comes early."

By this time, Karen felt she was losing ground with the conversation, and as Aunt Hattie left the room she could not resist a smile. Theresa came into the room to collect the tray and spoke to Karen who had resumed her own seat at the table, thoughtful and lingering over her coffee.

"That woman smart," said Theresa. "She does keep it up here." Theresa tapped her own forehead. "You does talk to she but nuthin' come out 'bout the family." Theresa looked down at her apron and gave it a tug with both hands. "Poor woman. She grieve and grieve 'cause she know things not right."

But Karen knew it would be wrong for her to question Theresa, particularly as she was a servant, so she hastily changed the subject.

"Have you seen Harvey, Theresa?"

"No, Miss Karen. That boy, he done come and gone."

Karen smiled and Theresa left the room shaking her head and talking to herself as was her habit.

Karen rested her elbows on the desk and let her head rest in her hands. Just for a few moments she allowed herself a re-run of the morning's events. Her curiosity was aroused. Her mind went back to Michael and his spontaneous welcome to the *Ibis* when she climbed aboard.

It had been such a beautiful morning, and the thought of his invitation for the whole day on Sunday made her heart sing. She was quite carried away. The Hammond's warning about not making a friend of Michael had completely skipped her mind.

At last she realised that she was wasting precious time and picked up her pen. I really must not indulge my imaginings, she told herself sternly. There are still an awful lot of books to get through. I have hardly started on them yet!

She worked steadily until lunch time then went through to the kitchen for a snack, as usual. As she opened the refrigerator she heard Theresa's clumpy footsteps behind her and turned to smile at her. There was a movement outside and Karen raised an eyebrow just as Tracy peeped round the door.

"Why doesn't she come in?" Karen moved as Tracy bobbed back.

Theresa shook her head. "She too much mischief today," she said, then laughed.

Tracy became bolder and hovered in the doorway.

"No you don't, Missy. Shoo." Theresa

waved her apron in a sweeping motion and Tracy dodged outside again.

"Have you seen Harvey this morning, Tracy?" Karen wanted to know.

"Uhu. He go down to swim. You want he?"

"Yes. Would you give him a message for me? Ask him to look in and see me when he comes up to the house?"

Tracy nodded and ran off, the pale soles of her bare feet flashing across the grass.

"What a nice child she is, Theresa."

Theresa beamed, then shook her head as she seemed to do every time she spoke. "She have a mischief in her," she said, wagging her head even faster and enjoying the pride she felt in her child.

Karen ate her salad lunch and returned to the library. Half an hour later there was a tap on the door and Harvey appeared. "You wanted me?"

"Yes, Harvey. Warren has invited me to go to Caroni swamp this evening and Mrs. Hammond has suggested you come with us."

Harvey frowned. "I bet Warren doesn't know that. He certainly won't want me along."

"Why ever not?"

He shrugged and looked embarrassed.

Karen was puzzled. "Don't you get on very well with each other?"

"Oh, it's not that."

"I'd very much like you to come, Harvey. In fact, I might add, if you don't, then I shan't go either."

He looked pleased. "In that case, I'll come. What time?"

"I don't know. He didn't say."

"Probably about six o'clock. It'll take an hour or so to get over there. I'll hang around."

"Good. Then I'll see you later," she replied, relieved, then turned her attention to her work.

At four o'clock, an hour later than usual, just as she was putting her desk in order, Warren came into remind her that they would be leaving for the swamps at six.

"Righto. I'll be ready in good time," Karen said, pleasantly, then added, "That was a good idea of your mother's to suggest Harvey comes with us."

Warren looked annoyed. "I hadn't bargained on that," he replied. "I've only planned supper for two."

"Oh dear! I'm sorry . . . but it was your mother's suggestion."

"I see. Then you think there is safety in numbers."

"I didn't think . . . "

"Obviously." He turned on his heel and strode from the room.

Karen was relieved that Harvey was coming with them. She could not explain why, but whenever she found herself alone with Warren she felt uneasy.

At five-thirty Karen had showered and dressed in dark blue slacks, a sleeveless navy blouse and navy cardigan, an outfit she felt might be sensible in the darkness of the swamp.

Harvey, true to his promise, was waiting at the water's edge as Karen and Warren walked down to the boathouse. Warren appeared to have forgotten his annoyance, and from the moment they stepped down into the pirogue, with Harvey jumping into the stern, Warren set out to charm her.

Karen's feelings about Warren were still ambivalent. So far he had been kind to her, but there was something about him she did not altogether trust, despite her wish to like him if she could.

The sea was calm and the air balmy, with only a hint of breeze. A perfect beginning to the evening. The light was good for another hour, and as Karen leaned over the side of the boat she saw that the water was a clear green. Below them was another world. Huge jellyfish went pulsating by, just below the surface, and further out still a small hammer-head shark was weaving in and out of a shoal of brightly coloured fish.

"What are they?" Karen was glad of something to use for conversation.

"Probably angel fish," replied Warren, without even bothering to look.

He set the controls and got out a bottle of white wine and some glasses. As he uncorked it he laughed. "You're a bit of a sobersides, aren't you? Cheer up, why don't you!"

"I'm sorry. I don't mean to be. Everything is so strange to me. You'll have to give me time."

"You've been here a week."

"Yes, I know." She bit her lip. "D'you

know what I find most difficult to adjust to?"

"What?"

"The smells. Everything *smells* so strange. I can't seem to get used to it."

"That's an odd thing to say. All countries have their own smells."

"Do they? I didn't know that. I've never been out of England before." She paused. "Food tastes different, as well. Bananas here have a warm sun-filled taste — quite different from those you buy in England."

"That's only because they are sun-ripened here, whereas for shipment they are picked in the green state."

"Flowers aren't the same, either. Your mother has lots of roses in her garden, but none of them have a scent. Roses in England are all so fragrant, each variety different. It's odd."

"Maybe the tropical vegetation is too strong for roses to compete with. What about tuberoses?"

"You mean those mauvey and white flowers that look a bit like orchids?"

"Yes."

"*They* smell so overpowering I can't get near them."

Warren laughed. "You *are* having a hard time. Have some wine. Perhaps it will help to deaden the pain."

Karen laughed too, but rather sheepishly. "Give me a few more days," she said, holding up her wine glass in a toast and looking to see if Harvey was doing the same.

But he was not. It appeared that he had not been offered any wine. Karen, about to mention the fact, changed her mind. Warren caught her unspoken question. "Do you want wine, Harvey?"

The boy shook his head. "I've brought some pepsi with me." Then he turned away and looked down into the water.

"More wine for the lady?" Warren's tone had a slight edge.

Karen shook her head. "Perhaps later."

Warren went back to the controls and Karen left the cabin to sit beside Harvey in the stern. She did not talk to him, but knew he was aware of her presence and once, unexpectedly, he turned to give her a companionable grin.

The steady chug chug chug of the boat

was soothing. It maintained its course across the calm sea until, in the distance, a line of dense green appeared on the horizon.

There were no other craft in sight. As they drew closer, Karen noticed that the light had begun to fade, and the dense green showed a tangle of deep dark roots that rose up out of the water. Thick black mud showed at the water line, and as the pirogue edged closer still she saw brilliant red-backed crabs scuttle away to hide in the murky depths. She shivered. The light was fading fast now, and the shadows caused by the mangrove trees had a sinister air about them.

Warren said, in a low voice, "We shall have to stay as quiet as possible if we want to see the birds without disturbing them. They are naturally shy. Get comfortable now. You'll find some cushions in the cabin. I'll have to manoeuvre the boat, but you'll be able to watch from where you are."

Karen nodded.

As Warren handled the controls he motioned to Karen to look to the west where the sun was setting in an orange and purple glow. It was the moment when she saw a large bird approaching, but as it was silhouetted black against the radiant background it was impossible to detect its colour and whether it was, indeed, a scarlet ibis. She made an effort to follow its flight, but it was lost amid the thick dark green foliage.

Warren now turned off the engine and, with the aid of a long pole, guided the pirogue into a narrow channel which penetrated the swamp even further. The silence was ghostly. Now and then Karen heard the suck and lap of the thick dark mud as it moved with the tide and the movement from the boat. It smelled dank and looked ugly, causing her to recoil.

Afraid to speak for fear of breaking the spell, she pulled her cardigan closer and sat motionless, except for the occasional necessity for ducking her head to avoid overhanging branches that came at her unexpectedly.

On they went. Darkness was falling fast now, and the glow in the west was a darkening rose red with a blue haze above it. A star twinkled above them, and then another and another, hanging over the swamp like lanterns. Now the eerie silence was broken by another sound — the croaking of frogs.

Warren eased the pirogue to motionless and crept into the stern to sit close beside Karen. He placed his arm along the strut behind her, a hair's breath from her shoulders. She felt herself tense.

Then all at once there was the sound of rushing and beating wings, and as she looked up, there were the birds, almost upon them and flying in low . . . the most beautiful scarlet birds she had ever seen. The ibis were coming in to roost. Their vibrant colour was breathtaking as their wings reflected the very last of the sun's rays. It took all Karen's self-control not to cry out. They settled in the foliage around the pirogue, and as she peered through what little light remained, she could see the insubstantial nests that formed the colony.

For spellbound minutes they all sat immobile, but the birds were restless as if aware of human presence. Some flew away to return again and again.

Warren's arm crept about Karen's shoulders and slowly and inexorably he drew her closer against his side. His arms grew stronger and stronger and Karen, wanting to resist his unwelcome advances, wanted to call out angry words at his spoiling of so perfect an experience. But because of the need to remain silent, and also very much aware of Harvey's presence, she could not. She had no option but to yield to his embrace against her inclination.

At last she wriggled free, but no-one spoke. Harvey never so much as turned his head. It was as if he knew what was going on and pretended not to.

Warren got up, quite coolly, whispering to Harvey, "Take the other pole and help me manoeuvre the turn."

The boy silently obeyed him, and as they moved into the open sea once more, he replaced the pole where he had found it then stood watching the water, arms akimbo, until Warren had returned to the cabin.

Karen looked about her. Now that they were no longer amid the dense foliage she saw that the whole landscape was bathed in bright moonlight.

Harvey turned to her. "Coming up on the roof with me?"

Surprised at his perspicacity, she replied, "Oh . . . can we?"

"Why not? I always do."

Karen turned to locate Warren, reluctant to let him feel that she was deserting him in her obvious rejection. He gave her a quick glance and said, "It's okay. I'll set the controls to slow and we can eat."

She watched him as he did so, then he lifted a picnic basket from beneath the cabin table and began sorting through it. Pleased at the prospect of supper, she put up a hand for Harvey to help her up onto the roof.

"Hold on," said Harvey. "Pass up a few cushions first."

She did as he suggested then clambered up beside him. "This is wonderful," she observed, looking across the sparkling silver sea. But Harvey was busy pulling the ring off a can of pepsi. "Umm," he conceded, "but I could do with a bite to eat."

"Coming up," called a voice from below as Warren handed them a paper plate each of fried chicken, salad and a buttered hops bread.

Karen leaned over the canopy. "Aren't you coming to join us?"

"No. I'd prefer to stay here. If you want some wine you can come and get it."

She ate her chicken and salad, feasting on the deep blue starlit sky, the beauty of the moon that cast a luminous glow over everything and the sparkling sea.

After some time, Warren called up, "Come and share a glass of wine with me," and Karen climbed down to join him. Harvey stayed where he was.

She accepted a glass of wine and they sat in the stern in silence until Warren said, quietly, "I *had* hoped we could have come alone. I wanted to take you on to a nightclub."

Surprised, Karen replied, "Sounds fun . . . but this has been a wonderful experience." She laughed. "I can't take in *everything* at once, now *can* I!"

He took her hand and led her into the cabin where he poured another drink for himself. Karen stood beside him and sipped her wine then set it down on the table as she idly watched him gather up the remains of their supper and pack it away in the basket.

Whether it was the wine that caused her to slip her guard she could not decide, but all at once she found Warren's arms around her, holding her so tight she could hardly breathe. His lips sought hers with a ferocity she had never known and she was frightened. She struggled in vain ... his lips closed on hers relentlessly and she was powerless to move.

Suddenly they heard Harvey's voice. "Hey! What's going on down there? Is there any more food? I'm still hungry." Quick as a monkey he swung down from above as Warren released Karen. He gave one look at Karen then nonchalantly came into the cabin, opened the picnic basket and helped himself to another piece of chicken and returned to the moon-deck, still munching.

Karen's face was flushed with anger and embarrassment. She made her way to the stern and sat down to recover from her trembling.

Warren brought her another glass of wine, but she declined it with a cold gesture. He sat beside her but she ignored him, and after a while he returned to the cabin and switched on the ignition. He set the controls and the pirogue went chugging towards Bucare. "Have I offended you?" he asked, as if he did not know.

Karen's temper flared. "Yes. You have." She was tight-lipped. "I wish you hadn't kissed me like that."

"But surely you knew it was bound to happen!"

"Of *course* I didn't. I'm not in the habit of kissing every man I meet."

"Except, perhaps, Michael Williamson, may be?" He laughed, mockingly.

She had no reply to that. How could he possibly know that Michael had kissed her? He must be bluffing.

She turned her back on him. He threw the half-empty bottle of wine overboard with an almighty splash and said, "That's that, then. I'm sorry I spoiled your evening." His tone was sarcastic.

Karen felt only a spark of contrition, but after all, he had been kind enough to bring her to the Caroni swamps; it was an evening she would always remember. "I'm sorry, too, Warren. Let's forget about it."

"It's very unlikely," he murmured. "But if it makes you any happier, I'll apologise." Some vestige of embarrassment flickered across his handsome features, and for a split second Karen wondered if she were making a lot out of nothing. As if he knew what she was thinking, he said, "Couldn't you have taken a kiss in the spirit it was given? It's only a moonlight picnic, you know."

But she did not reply.

Some time later she made an effort at conversation, asking Warren to tell her more about the Caroni swamps. "How far does it stretch?"

"It's about ten thousand acres altogether." But he sounded sulky.

"My! *That* big?"

"Don't bother with the chit-chat," he said. "You have rather dampened my enthusiasm for small talk."

Karen felt her colour rising again. He may have thought her a killjoy, but no matter how many times she thought back on the incident she was convinced he should not have behaved as he did. As an employee it put her in an invidious position.

When they finally got back to *Tabara*, Karen went straight up to her room, unhappy and confused. But when she got into bed she thought how perfect the rest of the evening had been. It was a pity that Warren had had to mar it with his ridiculous amorous behaviour. She would just have to try and see the funny side of it.

6

BY Friday morning Karen had systematically worked along the top shelf of the left hand wall and was contemplating starting on the second. She pulled the steps into the corner and climbed them, reaching out to take as many books as she could manage.

As she was about to climb down, a particular book further along the shelf caught her eye. She hesitated, then carried the books she already had in her arms to the desk and went back up the steps for another look.

She pulled out the volume she had noticed. Perusing it carefully she realised that she was holding a treasure. It was a rare edition of William Blake's 1793 print of *Gates of Paradise.*

Looking along the same shelf she saw that there was also an Erasmus Darwin, entitled *Zoonomia*, printed in 1794 – or was it 1796? She could not quite make out the correct date as the gilt on the leather had worn.

Then another volume caught her eye, and then another and another. She began to tremble with excitement and her legs were so wobbly she could hardly climb down the steps without falling. But . . . something suddenly alerted her not to divulge her find until she had written to Mr. Arnold for confirmation. He would have to advise her first, whether they were in fact valuable books. She might possibly be mistaken, though her intuition told her otherwise.

Hardly able to contain her animation at her discovery, she wasted no time in pulling out a sheet of paper. Then taking up her pen, she wrote:-

Dear Mr. Arnold,

The most exciting thing has happened. But before being completely carried away, I thought it would be a good idea to write to you first.

I have not mentioned my discovery to anyone, just in case I may be mistaken, but would you confirm that the following books are as valuable as I believe them to be:-

William Blake 1793
  Gates of Paradise
Erasmus Darwin 1794 – 1796
  Zoonomia
John Wolcot 1817
  Epistle to the Emperor of China
Walter Savage Landor 1836
  Poems. Pericles of Aspasia
Thomas Paine 1795
  First Principles of Government

Perhaps you will advise me on my best course of action.

Incidentally, there is something I don't quite understand. When Mrs. Hammond first wrote to you, I feel sure she said that her husband died after a long illness. But now that I am here, I understand that he was accidentally drowned. It seems rather strange that Mrs. Hammond should have made such a mistake. I thought you ought to know.

Thank you again for making the arrangements for my stay on Bucare so comfortable (financially, I mean). Also the trip over on the *Camello* – it was marvellous.

I hope to do a good job here. I am certainly enjoying it.

With very best wishes,
Sincerely,
Karen

Karen signed the letter and hunted for an airmail envelope but was unable to find one. She put the letter in her pocket, resolving to ask Warren if he would take her across to the mainland. Then she remembered that both he and his mother had gone across already. She would have to wait until he was going again. Perhaps the next day. Oh well, there was no desperate hurry. It could wait for a couple of days. Anyhow, perhaps she could ask Harvey to buy a packet of envelopes for her.

On second thoughts she decided to seek out Theresa. She was in her quarters, which were situated opposite the rear door from the kitchen. Karen knocked on the door and Theresa opened it to reveal a bed-sitting-room, nicely furnished, and the door of the adjacent shower and toilet which was open, so that Karen could see right in.

"Theresa, I'm sorry to disturb you, but have you such a thing as an airmail envelope?"

Theresa laughed. "I doesn't write no letters, Miss Karen. I got no cause to."

"Oh! I didn't think. How stupid of me." She hesitated. "Is there any way I can get over to Trinidad this afternoon?"

"You does want to post the letter?"

Karen nodded.

"Winston coming by here three o'clock. Maybe he take you, eh?"

"That would be fine. But how could I get back?"

"No problem. Winston coming back."

"Oh, I see. Thanks." Karen waved her hand. "I'll be in the library when he's ready."

Theresa nodded, and she was as good as her word, for a few minutes after three o'clock there was a tap on the library door and she appeared. "Winston ready now, Miss Karen."

Karen picked up her purse and left her work as it was, though she had been careful to replace the valuable books to their rightful place on the shelf. She had not as yet catalogued the rare editions, merely enumerated some of them in her letter to Mr. Arnold.

Winston had brought Tracy with him. It occurred to Karen to wonder if they might pass the Hammonds on their journey across to the mainland, but there was no sign of the pirogue and she felt relief; it might have been slightly awkward to explain her sudden whim.

The distance was covered in very little time. Being a much smaller craft with an outboard motor, Winston's boat cut along about four times as fast as the ponderous pirogue.

They drew up at the harbour wall between two fishing vessels and Winston indicated that he and Tracy would not be far away when she returned.

"Best get a cab to Frederick Street," he advised. "The Post Office is in Independent Square. Big black marble building. Can't miss it."

Karen looked puzzled.

"Any one cab stop for you. Just hold up the hand."

Karen did as Winston suggested and found herself seated in a large blue American car besides a plump woman with a cage of chickens on her knees. Sharing a cab in Trinidad was evidently full of surprises, it seemed, for in no time at all she was dropped in the main street of Port-of-Spain for just a few cents.

Frederick Street was crowded with colourful chattering people who spilled off the sidewalks with a nonchalance that defied belief. Cars honked and edged their way slowly through the throng and happy laughing faces were everywhere. Narrowly missed disasters were treated as nothing more than a joke.

Karen wandered happily up Frederick Street until she came to a department store. Inside, to her delight, it was air-conditioned. She found her way up the restaurant and ordered a cold drink, a recommended local non-alcoholic mixture they called a *Bentley special*, which turned out to be orange and lime juice with a dash of *Angostura bitters* with ice, and a marashino cherry impaled on a cocktail stick. She thought it was delicious and promptly ordered another.

She bought airmail envelopes on the ground floor, then found her way to the Post Office, the black marble fascia building in Independent Square, close by Frederick Street, just as Winston had explained.

Karen posted her letter then stood at the kerb where, to her surprise, a cab drew up before she had even raised her hand. Nothing could have been easier, and she was back at the harbour in no time, with Winston and Tracy looking out for her. She resolved to do it again, but to stay much longer next time. She loved the happy-go-lucky atmosphere of Trinidad and there would be so much to explore. Not only that, she could visit Frances, if she got the chance.

She returned to the library to find Laura Hammond waiting. Her expression was like a thundercloud and Karen suddenly felt guilty for no reason at all.

"Miss Warde," she demanded, "Where have you been this afternoon?"

"I went to post a letter, Mrs. Hammond."

"You went across to the mainland? How, may I ask?"

"Winston took me. In his fishing boat."

"And why, may I also ask, did you not let *me* do it for you?"

"I didn't write my letter until you had

been gone some time."

"Was your letter so very urgent, then?"

"I just wanted to let Mr. Arnold know how I was getting on. I should have written to him much sooner, to tell him I had arrived safely, I mean." She paused for breath. "It wasn't only that. I hadn't any airmail envelopes and it doesn't seem possible to find a shop on Bucare that sells them."

"I have plenty. You could at least have asked me first."

"It was after three o'clock, Mrs. Hammond. You gave me to understand that my time is my own after three o'clock."

Laura Hammond stalked towards the door. She was angry. At the door she turned. "Miss Warde, in future when you leave this island please inform me. I object to your sneaking off as soon as my back is turned."

Karen went a fiery red. "I certainly didn't *sneak*, Mrs. Hammond. I resent your remark. You have no right to speak to me like that."

"I have *every* right. Whilst you are here on Bucare you are in my employ and I am responsible for your safety."

Karen did not reply. She felt humiliated, and yet, in her own mind she had done nothing to deserve censure. Was there *no* pleasing her employer? She seemed to find fault with everything she did.

"One moment," said Laura Hammond, waiting until she had Karen's full attention once more. "My son and I are attending a beach barbecue this evening. I think it would be as well if you came with us."

"But you said I might do as I pleased with my leisure time!"

"Yes, I did. But I have changed my mind. It occurs to me to wonder whether you can be trusted in my absence."

Karen gasped. Never had she been spoken to in such an insulting manner. Hard put to it to think up a spontaneous reply, she held her anger in check and clenched her fists, saying, "No-one has ever spoken to me as you have, Mrs. Hammond. You have no reason at all to distrust me."

"Time will tell. You will come to the Barbecue tonight, anyway."

"Have I no choice at all?"

"No."

"Then I insist that I spend Sunday as I wish."

"Very well."

"What time shall I be ready this evening?" It was vital to get Laura Hammond's mind off Sunday.

"About nine o'clock. And wear something casual. It will be very informal."

Still fuming, Karen put her things away, doubly thankful she had remembered to replace the valuable books to their rightful places before she had left for her trip to the mainland. Her employer would doubtless have noticed them had she left them on the desk.

I am beginning to wonder whether I am sorry I ever came to Bucare, she thought, then abruptly changed her mind when she remembered the voyage, and Michael.

As she stepped down into the pirogue at nine o'clock that evening, she hoped that in her sleeveless blue linen dress and white crochet stole she was suitably dressed.

Laura Hammond was in white slacks, and what was locally known as a *hot shirt*, a shirt worn outside slacks with a brightly coloured design,

Warren was similarly clad, and Karen subsequently found that such an outfit was the standard wear for barbecues. However, the others appeared unaware that she was differently dressed.

Though the tropical night was heavenly and the gentle but capricious breeze off the sea took care of the mosquitoes, Karen was dubious as to whether she would enjoy the evening. The stars were limitless, and the moon made the water look like liquid silver as the pirogue chugged through the shining sea. She took a cushion up on the roof as Harvey had shown her when they went to Caroni swamp. She lay in the moonlight watching the sea and wondering where Harvey was. It appeared that he had not been invited.

As they rounded a point of land she could see a sheltered bay alight with lanterns and tables beneath umbrella shaped shelters which, as they drew closer, appeared to be thatched with banana leaves. There was a backdrop of tall palms, waving gently in the evening breeze, and along the shore a stretch of gleaming silver sand.

As they drew close to the shore there came the sound of laughter, and Karen could see figures silhouetted against a blazing fire in a huge brazier. Some guests were swimming, others were standing or walking around on the sand with drinks in their hands. A delicious smell wafted towards them, and when they had landed they saw that it came from the steaks set out on wire trays resting above the brazier which had now dispersed its flaming ferocity and the charcoal settled to an intensified glow.

Karen's spirits rose a little, though she wished she could have been already acquainted with at least some of the guests. She would probably be the only stranger. However, it was jolly atmosphere and she thought it possible, after all, that she was going to enjoy herself. She had made an effort to settle her differences with Warren, at least for the time being.

He took her by the hand and led her to a group of people. "Meet the princess," he said, then gave her name.

Karen's hair glowed in the firelight and people gathered about her, curious to meet the newcomer to the island. She laughed with pleasure as she was introduced and accepted a glass of champagne. "I hope I can remember all your names," she said.

"You will by the end of the evening, Princess. Drink up." Warren was masterful.

Karen let herself drift on the tide of merrymaking, and when supper was announced they queued up at a long trestle table for plates and cutlery then helped themselves to various accompaniments – crisp celery, black and green olives, iceberg lettuce, baked potatoes in their jackets. Then they crossed to the brazier, where each guest was asked, "Medium, rare or well done?" The sizzling steaks were mouthwatering.

They sat in folding chairs at the water's edge with their plates on their knees and Karen was aware of nothing but the good company, the food, the sea and the sky. She had no idea who her hosts were but did not like to ask. It would have been more interesting still if she could have met them, but it appeared that Laura Hammond had no intention of letting her do so.

She wondered if Michael might be

there, but though she looked among the guests for him she did not see him. Knowing how few people lived on Bucare she concluded that most of the people must have come over from one of the other islands, or perhaps from Trinidad. There were, in fact, several sailing boats moored nearby.

After supper they wandered on the beach, and somehow she and Warren got separated from the others. She realised afterwards that it had been his intention from the start.

"Let's walk up as far as the chapel," said Warren. "It looks good in the moonlight."

"The chapel? It looks to be quite a distance away." She was reluctant, once again, to be alone with him.

"Oh, come on. You'll find it interesting. It's a small fishermen's chapel, right on the edge of the sea. Built there over a hundred years ago."

"Is it used?"

"I believe so. Mostly when they get a bumper catch, or perhaps when things get difficult."

Walking was pleasant. Karen took off

her shoes and waded in the ebb tide. The water was warm and she loved the feel of the silver sand pushing up between her toes.

When they reached the chapel Warren indicated that they should go inside, but Karen was reluctant. It looked dark and forbidding to her, and she certainly did not relish being in there alone with him.

"Come on," urged Warren, his words slightly slurred from drinking so much champagne. "It's perfectly okay. I often come here."

Karen glanced back along the shore. "What about the others?" She was putting on her shoes.

"Who cares about the others?" he said, roughly. "Come." He gripped her hand so fiercely it was difficult for her to resist him. She felt alarm, objecting to his manner. How stupid I am, she thought, to have let myself get in this situation.

"Let go of my hand, please, Warren. I'm quite capable of walking without your tugging at me."

Suddenly, without any warning, he flung his arms around her, and before she could stop him he was kissing her fiercely — even more passionately than he had when they visited the Caroni swamp.

She was furious. She tried to pull away from him but he would not let her go. She dropped her purse and concentrated on fighting him off with both hands, but it was difficult as her arms were pinned to her sides.

She struggled and struggled, twisting her body this way and that, until she finally managed to bend her knee and give him a sharp kick on his shin.

He took his mouth away from hers to utter a violent oath, and that split second she managed to free herself as his hand flew to nurse his injury. In her wildest imaginings she would never have contemplated doing such a thing as kicking someone hard, but she was desperate, and if she did not show her disgust in some way there was no knowing how it might end.

Warren retaliated by slapping her across her face with the back of his hand. "You little vixen," he shouted at her.

She quickly took off her shoes again and ran as fast as she could back along the shore. Her face was bleeding where his signet ring had caught her cheek and tears were streaming down her face. It was fortunate that she had only had one glass of champagne and could run much faster than he could after the considerable amount of drink he had imbibed.

When she had covered about a hundred yards and was out of breath, she stopped and looked back. Mercifully he was not following her. He was merely standing looking out to sea. She knew that not only was he frustrated, but angry.

She made her way back to the barbecue and helped herself to a couple of paper napkins to clean herself up. She had her shoes, but her purse and crochet stole were somewhere along the shore. It was anybody's guess whether she would ever be able to recover them.

She kept in the background until she finally saw Laura Hammond make her way to the pirogue, then followed. Very soon afterwards Warren joined them. As he stepped over the side of the boat he threw Karen's purse and stole onto the seat beside her, but she said nothing.

It was two a.m. when they finally got back to *Tabara*.

Karen made a hurried retreat to her room, but it was a very long time before she got to sleep. She had been shocked at Warren's behaviour a second time. How *could* she cope with him? He was abominable.

Finally, after tossing and turning for an hour, she got out of bed and locked her door. She wanted no more unpleasantness.

The locked door gave her a degree of security, and at last she fell asleep. Mercifully tomorrow was Saturday, and on Sunday she would be seeing Michael. Or *could* she? The prospect of Michael seeing her bruised face dismayed her. How could she possibly explain what had happend? It would not be much good to hatch up some story about falling over. She was a hopeless liar, she knew, and would only forget and accidentally let out the truth some time later. If her face was unsightly tomorrow she would have to put off her date with Michael. Perhaps the bruise would be less obvious in the morning. At the moment it throbbed, and to comfort herself she fetched a soft towel from the bathroom and laid it against her face. Then exhausted both physically and emotionally, she turned on her side and fell asleep at last.

Karen's first thought on waking early on Saturday was to inspect her bruises.

She got out of bed and went across to the dressing-table. Putting her hand to her cheek to test how much it hurt, she looked into the mirror and gasped. The wound was very sore and considerably swollen. However, the gash that had bled so freely last night was already closed and healing, thought there was a very obvious bruise surrounding it. "Oh dear," she sighed aloud, "I can't possibly let Michael see me like this. It's too awful. What can I do? I'll have to get a message to him somehow."

There was a knock on the door. She went to unlock it then scampered back to her bed, pulling the sheet high up around her. She prayed that it was Theresa. It was. But if she hoped Theresa would not notice the bruise she was sadly mistaken. When she saw Karen's face she collapsed in a fit of laughter. Karen was completely taken aback.

"Oh Lordy, Miss Karen," she said, between laughter and tears, "She man bin beatin' she?" Her eyes danced with joviality.

Karen, although very surprised at the unexpected turn of events, suddenly caught Theresa's infectious humour and laughed with her, though she resisted telling what really happend.

When they had both stopped laughing, Karen said, "Please don't say anything to Mrs. Hammond, Theresa. I don't want to attract her attention to it."

"I swear, Miss Karen. But you is some funny." She wagged her head. "Let me get she breakfast, eh?"

Karen nodded. "Thanks. Just something simple, though. Nothing cooked."

"I fetch it to you."

When Theresa returned with a laden tray, Karen said, "Don't go, Theresa. I want to ask your help."

The maid, curious, shut the door and came back to the bedside.

"Theresa," whispered Karen, "do you know where Michael Williamson lives?"

"Sure I does." Theresa nodded solemnly.

"Would it be possible, do you think, to get a message to him? He's expecting to meet me down on the beach early tomorrow morning, but I can't possible let him see me like this."

Theresa started to giggle again.

"I'm quite serious, Theresa."

"Yes, Miss Karen. I knows. But you some funny."

"It doesn't feel very funny, Theresa," she said, sadly. "I was so looking forward to going sailing with Mr. Williamson tomorrow."

"Maybe it come better next Sunday."

"Perhaps . . . but can you get a message through to him for me?"

Theresa shook her head. "No need. Harvey can tell he tomorrow mornin' when he come."

"What will he say?"

Theresa grinned. "I think of somethin'."

"Thanks." Karen sighed and resigned herself to her disappointment. She could take time eating her breakfast now, but it was sickening to think how Warren had spoiled everything. Whatever had possessed him to treat her as he did?

Was it the champagne?

She thought over her own behaviour in order to satisfy herself that she had not led him to believe his attentions would be welcome. No, she was sure she had not: the reverse, in fact. She had been literally forced to go to the barbecue, and knowing full well that she was at a disadvantage, he had behaved despicably. She was resolved to accept no more invitations from Laura Hammond, for it was against Laura Hammond that her anger was really directed. Warren was of no account. She felt nothing for him except the abhorrence she had experienced when his lips were pressed against hers. She shuddered and made an effort to shake her mind free of it.

She sipped her orange juice appreciatively before starting on the pawpaw, then toast and marmalade and coffee. She looked forward to the pawpaw each day. It was so delicious served with a wedge of lime and fine cane sugar. It was something she would miss when she returned to London.

When she was dressed, the thought of facing Laura Hammond was distasteful, and she shrank from a further encounter with Warren, even though it would be inevitable some time later in the day.

"I think I will work today," she said aloud, to herself. "I'll get on with the job and finish it as quickly as I can."

Karen worked undisturbed until lunch time. Theresa, at her request, brought her in a tray of salad at one o'clock and she worked on again, right through the afternoon. It would soon be supper time.

She would have liked to go for a swim, but compromised with a shower. The bruise on her face was easing, but still showed rather markedly. She powdered over it as best she could and went down to supper.

She sat quietly at the table with the family, but there was little conversation. Warren, especially, avoided looking at her after an initial glance when she walked in and he realised with a shock the damage he had inflicted on her.

It crossed Karen's mind to wonder if Laura Hammond had noticed her bruised face, but as she said nothing Karen was relieved. The whole thing was best forgotten.

Harvey was absent, and Karen guessed that he was off on his own pursuits.

Her spirits were low as she thought about her disappointment. It would have been wonderful to sail in the *Ibis* again. That exquisite freedom and the sight and sound of the sails in the wind, a wind so tempered by the trade winds and almost warm, filled the soul with unspeakable joy.

When she returned to her room that night she gazed out over the sea and let her imagination take over. Imagination would have to console her. It was probable that she would never have the chance to experience such joy ever again. Laura Hammond would see to that . . . or Warren, perhaps.

7

FROM then on Karen breakfasted in her room each day. It was Theresa's idea sensing she might prefer to do so.

Karen had worked steadily for five days now. On the Sunday which she had been hoping to spend with Michael she worked all day, and the number of books she had listed had given her an impetus to keep to her decision to finish the job as quickly as she could and return to London. Her interlude on Bucare was becoming too fraught with difficulties for her to enjoy her stay at *Tabara*. It was obviously not possible that a good relationship could ever be established with Laura Hammond. From the very first she had shown antagonism towards her.

Karen sighed and picked up her pen to resume her task, thankful in the knowledge that she loved the job she had come to do. She looked up at the three walls of books with pleasure. Just the sight of them made her feel good. Even the room itself exhaled a friendliness, and she wondered why it should be so.

Towards lunch time, however, she became restless. She needed an outing, or perhaps a swim. Then it occurred to her that Trinidad might be more fun. Yes, that is what she would do. She had worked every day so far that week, so her conscience was clear. She put down her pen and went in search of Laura Hammond.

Laura Hammond was tending her orchids when Karen located her. She was unexpectedly friendly, and when Karen told her that she would like to visit Trinidad she made no objection. "Of course, Miss Warde. Warren will be only too pleased to take you."

Karen's heart tripped; she wanted to ask Winston the fisherman to take her. However, grateful for the lack of animosity, she swallowed hard and murmured her thanks.

Warren was down in the boathouse. He had only just returned from his daily trip to the mainland and was unloading the day's supplies. When Karen appeared, he looked up from his labours. "Anything we can do for our dedicated librarian?" he asked.

"Your mother has given me permission to go across to Trinidad. I was going to ask you to take me, but I didn't realise that you'd only just come back."

"No matter."

"Wouldn't you prefer me to ask Winston?" Karen was hopeful. She would have much preferred Winston's company. It would also be quicker.

"I think my mother would want *me* to take you," he replied, his lips firming. "Just give me ten minutes whilst I unload this stuff."

"Thanks. I'll come back later. I need to get my purse, anyway."

When she got back to the boathouse Warren was waiting for her. He turned on the ignition as she stepped down into the pirogue.

Out on the open sea she made an effort to be friendly, but as Warren responded only half-heartedly she moved out of the cabin to sit in the stern. In a way, she felt beholden to him. On the other hand, she had been forced into the situation, so what could she do?

Unexpectedly, he called to her. She approached him warily. What now, she wondered.

"How's the face?" He said it without looking at her.

"Improving," she replied.

"I'm sorry it happened," he said, then added, "but you brought it on yourself."

"Why! For heaven's sake?"

"There's something about you that gets me going," he muttered. "You're too damned attractive."

She ignored his comment and left the cabin to return to the stern. What *could* she have said?

When they reached the quayside on the mainland, Warren took her arm to steady her as she alighted on the steps then threw her the rope to secure it to a capstan.

"How long will you be?" he called. "Shall I come with you?"

"No. I want to look at the shops," she replied. "I'd rather be on my own."

He consulted his watch. "I'll meet you in the Angostura bar in two hours time."

"Where is it?"

"At the bottom of Frederick Street. You'll find it. Look for the sign . . . then you go up some stairs."

"I'd like to stay a little longer than two hours."

He shrugged. "I'll give you two and a half hours, but no more."

Karen unwillingly acquiesced then, mustering her assurance, walked across the tarmac to hail a cab. She very much wanted to visit Frances and Giles, but apart from the time limit Warren had stipulated, she had no idea where they lived. Everything conspired against her freedom.

As before, she found herself in a crowded vehicle, this time poked in the ribs by a guitar, but as the driver was so intent on rushing his passengers to their destination with the prospect of picking up ever more fares, she soon found herself in Frederick Street.

The place was alive with people of all nationalities, even to the point of bewilderment, with barely room to walk on the crowded pavement. Perhaps a tourist ship was paying call.

Never had she encountered so much back-slapping and chatter on such a hot afternoon. What could they all have to gossip about? Snatches of conversation were not very enlightening. They spoke the English tongue, but the words were in such an odd sequence as to make the meaning incomprehensible to her. She heard a tall dark flashily-dressed man say to a rotund smiling woman, "Is Eddoes. For every thousand you get he go give you a penny." What ever did he mean? If she had lingered to hear more she would have discovered that they were talking about Carnival. Carnival past and Carnival to come.

Her first call was to the Bank, and she was gratified to find that a note of credit had already been dealt with. She was handed a cheque-book and then she asked for some cash. It would be fun to do some shopping.

Looking about her, Karen saw that she was close by the large emporium where she had bought the airmail envelopes on her previous hurried visit. She decided she would first explore one or two Indian and Chinese bazaars then go back to the emporium where she would revel in the air-conditioning.

Her ears were unaccustomed to Indian music, and as she entered the bazaar of her choice its monotonous lilt carried her into an exotic mood so that she relaxed and searched her way through the racks of colourful shirts until she found one to her liking. It was pure silk and striped in cream and blue and mauve, and it delighted her. A pair of harem trousers in a toning shade of mauve beguiled her, and when she looked at the price tag was pleasantly surprised.

Lighthearted now, she took the goods to the check-out where a young Indian girl wrapped them caressingly in tissue and placed them in an attractive plastic carrier bag, giving Karen a smile as she thanked her for the purchase and hoped she would come again.

"I will," said Karen, impulsively. It was refreshing to hear a kindly world.

In the emporium she bought a one-piece bathing suit. It was no more than a streak of satiny gold, but Karen was feeling the lure of the tropics.

Much later, when it was time for her

to meet Warren, she came down to earth. She knew where the Angostura bar was; she had spotted the sign as she came out of the Bank.

About to cross the road, she noticed an Art Gallery with a particularly attractive landscape displayed in the window. Through the doorway she could see a number of fascinating pictures and was very drawn to looking at them whilst she had the chance. She glanced at her watch ... she could spare about ten minutes — it wouldn't hurt to keep Warren waiting for a bit.

The interior of the gallery was softly lit and appeared to be deserted. She found her way up a staircase, deciding to start at the top and work down.

She made her way from picture to picture and was enthralled by what she saw. There was a vividness about a number of modern paintings. She looked closely at one she liked particularly — a study in oils of a lush cane field with the sea in the distance and a promontory that reached out into the water. The sky was a deep mauvey-blue, and the jade-green sea washed the silver sand giving an impression of imperceptible motion. She bent over to read the signature. It read, *Leonard da Vinci.* She smiled to herself. What an impossibly perfect name for an artist.

About to turn away she noticed a picture which had been placed with its face against the wall, on the floor. Curiosity drove her to take at look at it. She turned it round, and for a split second she was confused . . . it was quite obviously the twin picture in the study at *Tabara.* What on earth was it doing here?

At the moment a large dark-skinned man with a handsome beard came silently up the staircase and stood beside her. He was in ethnic dress and his presence was slightly intimidating, but when he spoke his eyes shone and his voice was gentle.

Karen drew in her breath.

He said, "You are interested in the hunting scene?"

She nodded. "I must admit that I am more surprised than anything. This particular painting is one of a pair. Perhaps you have it here for cleaning?" She turned to confront him. "Mr . . . ?"

"The name is da Vinci."

"Oh," gaped Karen, "then you are the artist who painted those beautiful landscapes downstairs?"

Leonard da Vinci momentarily closed his eyes and made a slight bow. "The very same," he said.

Karen replaced the hunting scene as she had found it and walked towards the staircase. "May I come back in a few days' time and have a better look round? Unfortunately I have someone waiting for me."

Leonard da Vinci spread his large hands and smiled. "Surely."

Karen, embarrassed now, left the gallery and crossed the road. She hurried down to the corner of Frederick Street and found her way up the stairs to the Angostura bar where Warren was waiting for her. She had already resolved not to mention the hunting scene she had just discovered. After all, it was none of her business.

As she got to the top of the stairs a cold blast of air met her. She shivered. The air-conditioning was several degrees colder than anywhere else, but Warren laughed at her discomfort. He asked what she would like to drink.

"A Bentley special, please."

He raised an eyebrow. "So you have sampled one of the local favourites already!"

She nodded. He ordered a rum punch for himself and the drinks were brought to them.

Karen drank thirstily; she was anxious to leave.

"What's the hurry?" He lolled in his seat and observed her through half-closed eyes.

She shrugged and crossed her arms to run her hands up and down her bare arms. "I'm cold," she said.

He made a gesture of impatience then hastily finished his own drink and stood up. "You're not going back to *Tabara* yet," he announced.

Karen, alarmed, jumped to her feet, open-mouthed and about to protest.

He held up a restraining hand. "Bear with me," he said, then giving a sardonic smile moved across to the bar to pay the bill.

She went towards the door and hurried into the street where she stood soaking up the warmth. She had been chilled to the bone in the bar upstairs.

When Warren joined her she began to walk in the direction of the quayside, but he called her back. "We aren't going that way, yet. I want to take you somewhere."

"Where?" She was both agitated and irritated at being so much at the mercy of his whims.

"You'll find out," he said, then hailed a cab.

Almost before she knew what was happening a cab had stopped and she was firmly manoeuvred into it, with Warren slipping in beside her. Upset now, she was very much aware that to protest would get her nowhere.

"Macqueripe," Warren told the driver, then added, "and don't pick up any more fares on the way."

The driver nodded and drove on up Frederick Street. He turned left at the first traffic lights and proceeded along the western main road that followed the coast.

As they left the built-up areas and beyond Carenage village, the scenery changed. First they passed a huge pink wooden structure that jutted out into the sea, all rosy from the bauxite dust, used in the manufacture of aluminium. Barges and ships, some from Venezuela where the ore came from, stood by, waiting to unload or reload as processing dictated.

Then all at once the sea was the dominant feature. There was a wide sweep of shoreline, than as wooded slopes on the land side appeared, the road swept inland again between tropical vegetation. Cacao shade trees full of lilac-pink pea-shaped flowers, and others of more modest stature bearing bright yellow red-eyed flowers and heart-shaped leaves, specimens once brought to the West Indies from an obscure Amazon valley. Karen was eager to question Warren, but the cab was travelling too fast for him to be very specific.

Grass verges now framed the road ahead, and on her right, Karen caught sight of a tiny white church nestled closely into a huddle of trees.

About a mile further on they came to a stretch of tarmac with several large houses set about in the vicinity and steps leading up to a high pale stone building. Warren said, "Here we are," and the cab driver pulled up. Karen got out of the cab and Warren paid the driver, asking him to return later, but she did not catch what time.

Apprehensive now, she had no idea what she was in for. At first she began to worry and her spirits plummeted, then anger flared. Once again Warren was behaving in a completely arbitary way, with no regard to her feelings. As the cab drove away, she stood her ground and stamped her foot. "How *dare* you treat me in such a peremptory way!"

He stared at her and she glared back at him, still standing her ground and hoping for an explanation.

He put his hands in his pockets, walked round in a circle, came to a stop facing her and said, "Why are you so unreasonable? This is a good place to come. Why can't you be more appreciative? I'm only trying to give you a good time."

Unrelenting, she answered, sharply, "You don't even give me a choice. I'm furious at the way you've hi-jacked me out here without a word of explanation."

"Calm down. You could at least be gracious enough to sample what I've planned." He went a few steps and waited for her to follow.

Karen bit her lip. She felt not angry but confused.

"Come on. Give it a trial. I won't eat you." He grinned. "Come on," he repeated. "Let's have a swim and cool off." He turned and walked on up the steps.

She followed him, reluctantly. Her irritation went with her, but as she got to the top of the steps and went through the glass doors that he was holding open for her, she was so surprised she forgot to be angry.

A vast mosaic floor stretched right across the area in front of them to a low balustrade which ran in an oval, framing the edge of nowhere. Beyond and below was nothing but sea — deep blue on this side of Trinidad. Warren turned to watch her response. She was so impressed that her anger melted like a snowflake touched by the sun.

Relieved at her change of mood, he beckoned her to follow him across the mosaic floor. She nodded, but first she looked about her. At that time in the afternoon the whole area was deserted.

A sudden raucous sound made her look up. A large gaudy macaw, bright red, yellow and blue, was climbing about on the roof of an orchestral pavilion. Using his beak and his feet he was awkwardly manoeuvring his way to his objective yet protesting between each move. She could not decide what the bird was trying to achieve because as soon as he reached the end of the roof he looked down at her and squawked then repeated the process to get back to where he had started from. Karen laughed and followed Warren across to the balustrade to gaze at the scene below. Now she knew where everybody was — on the beach.

He led her to some steps. About a hundred of them, carved out of the solid rock of high cliff, and quite dizzying to descend until she noticed the handrail. Without thinking, she gladly made her way down, with Warren following. "Is it a private club?" she asked him.

He nodded.

Half way down was a wooden seat on a curve, with a cleft in the rock to look out to sea. Karen hesitated, but Warren went on down, so that she followed lightly behind him.

At the foot of the steps the beach of pale golden sand stretched either way and was an entity, inaccessible except by sea. At the extremities it was backed by shade trees, but in the centre, bathing huts were set into the foot of the cliff and an elevated board walkway with a handrail ran along in front of them. Warren led her to a cubicle. "You first," he said.

Karen entered the cubicle and turned to smile at him. "How do you know I've brought a swim suit?"

"I watched you buy it," he said. "That was what gave me the idea of bringing you here."

"You *followed* me?" She frowned.

He nodded, unabashed.

She clicked her tongue good-humouredly. How could she spoil such a promising afternoon? She closed the cubicle door and changed into her swimsuit. When she emerged Warren was placing folding chairs close to the water's edge, but she ran straight into the sea, aware that he was watching her.

The warm water was heaven and the

feel of it on her body was sensational. She swam steadily out to sea, but not beyond where two other swimmers were.

It was only a few seconds before Warren joined her. She pointed to a distant dark fin. "Is that a shark?"

Warren laughed. "Just an innocent horse-mackerel," he replied.

Karen swam away, but he followed her. "By the way," he said, as he caught up with her, "I like the swimsuit."

"Thanks," she replied, then treading water, she asked, "How long do you intend keeping me here?"

"Have you any complaints, then?" He grinned.

"No. It's beautiful. I only want to know where I stand."

"I thought we might stay on awhile. They usually put on a good supper later in the evening."

"But how can I let your mother know where I am? Can I telephone her?"

He laughed.

"What's funny?" She felt cross again, tired of guessing games.

"There aren't any telephones on Bucare. It's too small. Surely you could have worked that out for yourself."

Karen tossed her head and swam off again. He's impossible, she thought, making her way further down the shoreline to a group of shade trees and an inviting patch of virgin sand. But just as she was making her way out of the sea, two people came out from between the trees. They were carrying chairs and set them up in the very place she was making for.

To her surprise, the dark-headed girl waved. Puzzled, Karen hesitated, wondering who they were. Then, as the tall man turned to face her she recognised Giles and ran to them.

Frances stared at her. "What are you doing *here*?"

"I was forced into coming," replied Karen.

"Oh dear!" Frances turned to look at Warren as he scuffed along the sand towards them.

"So, we meet again," he opened, obviously less than keen at the encounter.

"Quite a surprise," replied Giles. "We often come here. I wonder we haven't seen you before. Warren Grant, I believe you said your name was."

Warren merely nodded.

Frances gestured to Karen and drew her away from the men. They strolled along the beach.

"Let's go into the sea," said Frances. "We can talk there." She slipped off her beach robe to reveal a brilliant multicoloured swimsuit with no pretence at modesty. "Come on," she called, racing for the sea and striking out into the crawl.

Karen followed, doing the breast stroke, and when they were parallel Frances wanted to hear all about *Tabara* and how the catalogue was progressing.

It must have been obvious to Frances that Karen was far from happy working for Laura Hammond, for she remarked on her somewhat deflated attitude. "What's the trouble, infant?"

Karen turned on her back to float. "I don't know," she replied, then added, "except that Laura Hammond can't stand the sight of me."

Frances trod water beside her. "Have you seen Michael again?"

"Only once. He took Harvey and me for a brief sail before breakfast one morning. There's something weird going on. I've been told by Laura Hammond that Michael is unwelcome at *Tabara*, but Harvey denies this. It's the other way round, he says. Michael will never come *there*."

"That's odd." Frances frowned. "Listen, Karrie. If you *are* in any difficulty at any time, come to *us* . . . you'd be very welcome."

"How do I find you?"

"Easily. We're the first house in La Fantasie. It's just around the corner from the Savannah. Any cab driver will know the way."

"Thanks, but I hope it never comes to that. But *I would* like to pay you a visit soon. I love coming across to Trinidad."

"Pop in *any* time. We've *got* to keep in touch." She paused. "Now let's sit on the beach for a bit. I don't like to spend too long in the water. I'm a bit scared of jellyfish. I got stung by one last time we came."

They went back to where Frances had dropped her beach robe to find that Giles was waiting for them.

"Where is Warren?"

"Gone to change."

"Oh, then I had better do the same. When he comes back, that is."

Karen was nervous. It stemmed from her fear that Warren might be unpleasant to Frances and Giles in some unexpected way. However, the rest of the afternoon passed peaceably enough and she was relieved when Warren offered to buy drinks for everyone.

Climbing back up the hundred or so steps was exhausting after swimming and lazing on the beach, but when they reached the top and saw the (now) floodlit terrace come into view, Karen's spirits rose.

All that was visible beyond the parapet was the dark blue of the sea merging into the darkening night so that the stars lit up the heavens. The sound of the waves breaking on the sand was only just audible now, for the steel band had taken over. Karen could quite easily have drowned herself in the sound of it, and she knew then that the lure of steel band music would never leave her.

She looked across to the music pavilion where six Trinidadians were beating out a haunting calypso called 'laziest man'. The music throbbed through her veins and she was hardly able to restrain a wild impulse to move her limbs to the seductive rhythm.

Chairs and tables were set for dining, but the centre of the terrace was clear for dancing.

Karen, still carrying her parcels, moved as if in a dream until Frances drew her attention to her shopping bags. "You can leave your things in the cloakroom, you know."

Karen nodded vaguely and Frances steered her in the right direction. When they reached the cloakroom she impulsively showed Frances the outfit she had bought that morning.

"Gorgeous," pronounced Frances. "Wear it this evening. Go on. Put it on." She gave Karen a push. "Wake up," she said, "you look as if you are having a vision."

"I am," Karen replied, biting her lip. "Oh Frances! Michael's here. I've seen him."

"Yes, I know."

"You didn't tell me."

"I knew you'd find out soon enough. Go on . . . change into your new togs. They'll make you feel good."

"You'll wait for me?"

"Of course."

When they emerged they found Giles and Warren sitting glumly at the same table, though the atmosphere improved as the two girls joined them. Warren's eyes opened as he took in Karen's changed appearance, and she knew she looked attractive.

After they had had supper Giles asked her to dance and she was pleased enough to do so, but her thoughts went to Michael. Had he seen her, she wondered. She looked for him but he had disappeared. She had almost given up hope of seeing him again when she felt a tap on her shoulder. She turned quickly to see Michael smiling down at her. "Hi there, Giles," he said, though his eyes never left Karen.

Her heart flipped. He was dancing with the blonde girl she had seen him with before. He introduced her as Rosemary.

Now her heart would not stop thumping. It was impossible to hide her feelings of pleasure at seeing him again. A slight respite was afforded her as he began chatting to Giles whilst the two pairs circled each other and Rosemary smiled and said, "Why don't we go over to the parapet? We can talk there."

"Good idea," said Giles, hesitating as he looked around for Frances and Warren. But they were nowhere to be seen, and for that Karen was grateful. Heaven only knew what fuss Warren might make if he knew she was with Michael Williamson!

They walked across to the balustrade and Michael changed his position to stand beside Karen. He whispered. "I was disappointed. What about *this* Sunday?"

"You mean, come sailing?" She caught her breath.

He nodded.

"I'd love to. But it's so difficult to get away."

"I gathered it was something like that," he said, thoughtfully. "The safest plan is not to say anything in advance but to leave a note letting them know where you've gone."

"But . . . " Karen suddenly caught sight of Warren and Frances converging, and she could not finish what she was intending to say. Rosemary winked at her and she wished she knew exactly what the relationship was between them. Rosemary did not appear to have any objection to Michael's attentions to another girl.

Warren was frowning. "It's time we were getting back to *Tabara*."

She found it easier to nod. It would not do to inflame him. The prospect of the journey back to *Tabara*, alone with him, was quite a hurdle as it was.

Before they left, however, she decided to return to the cloakroom and change into her other clothes. Frances followed her, and when they were completely alone she complimented Karen on her new outfit. "Thank's Frances. My confidence could do with a boost."

Frances grinned. "I don't know why. I saw the way Michael looked at you."

"But we weren't with him more than two minutes!"

"Long enough! Come along. You'd better not keep your gaoler waiting."

Fortunately for Karen, the journey back to *Tabara* was uneventful, and though Warren was uncommunicative, the silence between them was not unpleasant. She was relieved.

She said goodnight to him at the top of the stairs and tiptoed to her room, locking her door. Then she undressed, got into bed and lay there going over the events of the day. She was drowsing off when she heard a soft knock on her door.

"Who is it?" she whispered, terrified that it might be Warren.

"Theresa here, Miss Karen. I have a message."

Karen opened her door and ushered her in. "A message, you say?" Her heart beat faster.

"It Mr. Michael. He want you be ready on Sunday mornin' early. Seven o'clock. Same place like last time only you couldn't go."

Karen's heart leapt again. "Oh, good. Thanks for waiting up to tell me tonight."

"You pleased, eh?" Theresa giggled.

She nodded. Then with a conspiratorial exchange of gestures, Theresa let herself out. This time her feet were bare, so that she made no sound.

So, thought Karen, Michael must have sent the message much earlier that day.

Seeing her tonight, unexpectedly, and repeating the invitation, had not been an impulse. That pleased her.

What could *possibly* stop her from going *this* time?

8

SUNDAY came at last. Karen was ready and waiting long before sun-up and before anyone else in the house was stirring.

But first she must write the note about her absence for the day — not that she intended to reveal where she was going.

That done, she picked up the rush basket containing a few things she might need for her day's outing, carefully opened her bedroom door and closed it quietly behind her.

She tiptoed down the stairs and, after placing the note on the hall table, reached the side door of the house with a sigh of relief. The thought that someone might still prevent her from spending the day with Michael terrified her.

She tried the handle of the door. Mercifully it was unlocked; no doors on the island were ever locked at night. She supposed that on such a small island, where everybody knew everybody else, it was an unnecessary precaution.

She let herself out quietly and cautiously made her way down to the shore between the high hibiscus hedges and past the boathouse down to the edge of the sand where the water was lapping gently at her feet. A shiver of excitement ran over her as she spotted the *Ibis* riding at anchor, and then Michael waving to her to wait where she was.

He climbed over the side of the ketch and rowed across to her in the dinghy. To use the outboard motor would have resulted in alerting the household.

Today she was wearing blue jeans, a tee shirt and plimsolls, and she knew that Michael noted her apparel with approval. His eyes went to hers, but he made no comment – just held out his hand to her as she stepped into the dinghy. Then smiling, he took up the oars and rowed them both to the ketch.

As she sat there, gripping the sides of the small craft, she found she could not help observing how magnetic Michael was. This morning he was wearing black cotton slacks and a black turtle-neck sweater, and his tousled blond hair shone in the morning sun. Karen's heart pumped hard to beat down her excitement, but without success. She was sure she could have danced on the water given half a chance.

When they were both on deck and the dinghy secured, Michael leant forward and, putting both hands on her shoulders, kissed her forehead. "Welcome aboard," he said. Then turning, he beckoned her to follow him.

He took a guy rope and let out the mainsail, winched up the anchor and the *Ibis* moved towards the open sea.

It was a perfect morning. A fine breeze, just enough to take the ketch into the wind until *Tabara* was no longer in sight. Five minutes later he hauled down the sail again and dropped anchor. "We'll have breakfast now," he said.

They went down into the cabin where a simple breakfast was set out on the table. He took her rush basket from her and put it on the seat beside her. She felt completely at ease.

The excitement of the day before them made her quite light-headed and her anticipation was high.

Michael unplugged the coffee-pot and set it down on the table.

"Incidentally, before I forget," Karen began. "I had a strange experience two days ago."

"Strange?"

"Yes." She hesitated. "I was in Frederick Street having a browse in an art dealer's when I discovered a hunting scene that looked astonishingly familiar. It was propped against the wall on the floor. I couldn't understand it until it came to me . . . it was the partner of the one in the library at *Tabara*."

"That's odd. What made you think it was a partner? There are already two hunting scenes in the library."

"Only one . . . well, there's an empty space . . ." she began. "No," she corrected herself, "not exactly an empty space, but a faded patch on the wall which corresponds in size to the hunting scene on the left hand side of the window wall. Another picture has been hung on the faded patch, but it's something entirely different, and in size."

"So that's it. Laura must be trying to sell."

"Are you upset, Michael?"

"Yes. Very upset. I think my father would be, too, if he knew."

"What can you do about it?"

"I don't know. But I think I'll have a word with that art dealer and see whether he has been offered anything else."

"I'm so sorry." Karen hesitated. "Michael, I think there is something else you should know. I believe Mrs. Hammond intends to sell all the books in the library. There are four thousand, and I have been asked, particularly, to leave a column for valuation purposes."

He looked angry. He grappled with his feelings for a few moments then said, quietly, "Thanks for telling me. I thought something like this might happen, but I don't quite know what I can do about it."

"It's a marvellous collection, you know. There are some extremely valuable books there." I should like to tell him about the first editions, she thought, but I had better keep quiet. Mr. Arnold would advise me to, I expect.

"I will give the matter some thought." He looked up at her and smiled. "I suggest we forget everything to do with *Tabara* for today. I want you to enjoy it." Then he poured coffee for two.

Karen said, "Where's Harvey?"

"I didn't invite him. I wanted to be alone with you for part of the day." He sat down at the table so that he was facing her, then passed her a basket of mixed croissant and brioche and pointed to the butter and preserves. "Let's eat."

Karen needed no further invitation.

After they had breakfasted, Michael set the sails to north-east, slightly against the wind so that they were tacking in the direction of the mainland. They stood at the helm together.

"Are we going to Trinidad?" asked Karen.

"Just to pick up a couple of people." He grinned and looked down at her to watch her expression. It registered disappointment. She admitted to herself that she had hoped to be alone with him for the whole day. Then she remembered Rosemary. What about Rosemary? She just managed to maintain her composure, however, although several times she caught Michael looking at her with an amused expression. Was he laughing at her?

They were now drawing near to the harbour. Karen saw two people waving. They looked familiar, and once again it turned out to be Frances and Giles. She waved back to them then turned to Michael, who said, "Are you pleased?"

She nodded. "Oh yes. Are they coming with us?"

"Uhu. They often come over to Bucare. This visit happens to coincide with yours."

She stood at the rail whilst Michael dropped anchor about thirty yards from the harbour wall and got into the dinghy to fetch them.

As soon as Frances was on the deck of the *Ibis* she threw her arms around Karen, saying, "Who let you out?"

"I'm playing truant," laughed Karen.

"And enjoying yourself, no doubt." She glanced at Michael, who grinned.

Giles sedately shook hands and the four all began talking at once. Michael set the sails for Bucare again and, with the wind behind them now, away to the offside of Bucare, away from *Tabara*.

On the leeward side of the island the scenery was even more breathtaking. The flowering trees covered the higher slopes, and from the foot of the hills sugar cane grew in a swathe almost to the beach. Karen was reminded of the da Vinci painting, except that this was the real thing, with the warm scent of the sugar cane pervading the breeze.

Only one house was visible, and that was right up in the hills. Karen wondered idly who lived there. She could see a rough track leading from it, threading its way down the slopes in and out of the flowering trees, eventually appearing at the water's edge close by a jetty which the *Ibis* was making for.

Giles took down the sails and with one hand on the wheel Michael steered the ketch alongside the jetty and secured it.

Karen asked no questions but simply followed the others. Once, as they started to walk up the track, Michael put a protective arm around her. He did not repeat the gesture, however, but for the remainder of the day Karen imagined she could feel his arm still resting on her shoulder and wished it true.

As they continued to climb she found the going hard, but the others appeared not to notice how steep it was.

At length they reached the house and were met by Rosemary, first seen with Michael when she arrived and then at the rail of the ketch, then later at Macqueripe. She was obviously on familiar terms with him. Where did she fit in? Karen concluded that she was either his fiancée or his wife, but secretly hoped she was neither.

Then around the corner of the house an elderly good-looking man appeared. He was tall though slightly stooped and wore an old-fashioned panama hat with a wide brim and an immaculate light cream suit. He came tap tap tapping along the terrace with a silver topped malacca cane. He should have looked out of place, but instead, he lent the house a gracious air, and indeed, it was a beautiful home.

Almost a 'folly' in its setting among the trees, it was pearly-white, with smooth columns in the classical style, and the white painted wrought-iron work forming the four balconies was as intricate as lace.

"Where on earth have you been, Father?" Karen heard Rosemary exclaim. "I looked everywhere for you."

"Oh, here and there," he replied, provocatively. "I don't have to account to you for my actions, young woman."

"I know that. But you are exasperating. I think you purposely hide from me. I can never find you when I want you."

"Well, I'm here now."

"Yes. So you are." Rosemary was obviously well used to the game he played.

He now came forward to meet Frances and Giles, yet there was no formality. It was as if they had never left after their previous visit.

But with Karen it was different. He looked at her intently, then taking both hands after hooking his cane over one arm, said, quite seriously, "So this is Karen."

Michael said, "Yes. This is Karen."

"Welcome to *The House*," said Rosemary.

"Thank you for inviting me," replied Karen.

"Oh, I didn't invite you – Michael did.

But you are none the less welcome."

No clue. Nothing. Karen told herself to forget the matter and just enjoy herself. Which was what she did from that moment on.

First she asked about the flowering trees, and Giles was pleased to enlighten her. The pink blossom she had seen from a distance was on the Poui trees, and legend had it that the rains never came until the Poui has flowered three times in succession.

"Is that really true?" she asked.

"It usually works out like that," replied Giles. "All I can say is that it is very good timber – about twenty to thirty kilos per cubic foot. Also," he added, "particularly the yellow Poui. The wood is usually called *greenheart.* Have you ever heard of it? It's one of the toughest woods there are – second only in density to the *Lignum Vitae* – a single cubic foot of which may weigh anything from sixty to eighty kilos."

"Oh, *really*!" protested Frances, who was within earshot. "Don't crowd the poor girl with technicalities. She only wants to know the names of the various species so that she can air her knowledge when she gets back to England."

Karen laughed. "Yes, don't get too technical, please. I shan't be able to remember *everything* you tell me. But I *would* like to know how long the poui trees will stay in bloom like they are now."

"Until about May."

"From here I can see some gorgeous orangy-red trees. What are they?" She pointed.

"Flamboyant, I expect. They bloom about the same time."

"And the blue?"

"Some are the trees I was talking about just now – *Lignum Vitae.* The others are probably *Jacaranda.*"

Karen gazed across the hills for some time, lost in reverie. "Tell me" she said, "how did such a wonderful collection of flowering trees come to be planted here in the first place?"

"Ah," joined in Rosemary. "You had better ask my father about that."

"Yes, Uncle Paul," chipped in Michael, "how about it?"

(So, thought Karen, that is the mystery

solved. Rosemary and Michael must be cousins.)

The old gentleman, who had been listening intently, looked up and focussed his eyes on Karen. After a long pause, he spoke slowly. "My grandfather planted them in between timber trees that were already growing there, then the timber trees were felled for building the house. My grandmother made sure that for every tree that was felled, another was put in its place. There was no stopping her. She planted more and more after that – as many varieties as she could collect. We have only to sit here on the terrace and enjoy their beauty to be reminded of her love for all growing things." His words had a quietening effect on them all. Karen took a deep breath as if she felt a great relief for their preservation over the years. At last, she said, quietly, "I know exactly how she must have felt."

"Come into the house," said Rosemary. "I'm sure you could all do with a cold drink. Frances, will you show Karen the usual offices and I'll get organised."

Frances beckoned to Karen and led the way upstairs to a well appointed bathroom.

"How's it going at *Tabara*? You seem to have regained your perkiness."

"That's because I've escaped for the day," she replied, flippantly.

"Why don't you like it there?"

"I like the work. Very much. It's . . . oh, I don't know . . . a bit sinister. I'm not wanted there, I'm sure, but they are stuck with me now until I've finished the job."

"Well," said practical Frances, "you *are* only there to do a job, after all. What did you expect? To be accepted into the bosom of the family?"

"No . . . not exactly . . . it's . . . it's a bit more than that . . . a constant feeling of hostility, I think."

"You must have done something to upset them."

"Not as far as I know . . . except being friendly with Michael. That seems to insense them for some reason."

"It doesn't appear to stop you, I notice."

"No," admitted Karen, "but surely I can please myself who I associate with on my days off."

"Umm. But . . . "

"What were you going to say?"

Frances looked straight into Karen's eyes. "You know, I suppose, that Michael is the one person whom they *would* resent your being friendly with."

"Why?"

"He knows too much about them."

"What do you mean?"

"Well, he's the one person in the world who knows what *really* happened to Arthur Hammond."

"You mean . . . that business about being drowned?"

Frances nodded.

"Then it's true," said Karen, biting her lower lip.

"Yes. But there's not much anyone can do about it. No witnesses. None at all . . . except, of course, Michael."

"*Michael?*"

"I believe Michael saw what happened. That's why he won't go near the place any more."

"I thought it odd that Mrs. Hammond should have told Mr. Arnold that her husband had died after a long illness."

"Who is Mr. Arnold, for goodness sake?"

"My employer. Back in England. He

owns the bookshop where I work."

"Oh." Frances paused. "Does he know the truth?"

"Not exactly. I merely mentioned in my letter to him that there was some discrepancy between what Mrs. Hammond had said and what I had heard."

"You actually wrote that in a letter?"

"Yes."

"My God! You'd better be careful what you write in letters. Laura Hammond wouldn't be above reading the replies before you get them. She's a pretty ruthless character, from what I hear. You had better watch out."

"What about Warren?"

"I don't know. You know I don't. When we first met him at the airport, if you remember, he didn't know which of us was Karen Warde."

"Of course. I'd forgotten."

"You *could* ask Michael, I suppose."

"No, I couldn't do that."

Frances grimaced. "We had better go down. They'll be missing us."

Karen felt distinctly uncomfortable and began to wish that her job was even closer to completion. Although, if it were, it would mean leaving Bucare, and she was already in love with the island . . . or was it Michael she was in love with? She pulled her thoughts together and followed Frances down the stairs.

The remainder of the day was spent in delightful tranquility. Giles gave Karen a conducted tour of the gardens and she learned about many more plants and shrubs. *Ixora, Queen of Flowers, Thumbergia, Gloriosa, Oleander* . . . the island was a tropical paradise.

After supper, Michael indicated that it was time to leave.

Rosemary and her father waved to them from the terrace as they made their way down the track, or trace as it was locally known.

It was almost dark when they were on board the *Ibis* once more, and the moon had already replaced the sun.

They sailed back to Trinidad in the moonlight, and once again Karen stood at the rail, enraptured with the beauty of the tropical night.

Frances and Giles disembarked on the quayside and once again Michael set sail for Bucare. Karen watched him, fascinated at the efficient way he dealt with the ketch. Each manoeuvre he made gave Karen the feeling that the boat was responding to him personally.

When he had made sure that all was well, he came and stood beside her. She kept still, afraid by word or deed of betraying her feelings. She knew, without doubt, that she was deeply in love with Michael.

He went into the cabin and fetched her cardigan from the rush basket and placed it around her shoulders. She turned to smile up at him, and in the moonlight he could see that her eyes were shining. He wanted to take her in his arms and hold her close, but somehow the time was not quite right.

Karen gazed out over the shining water and he placed his hand gently over hers. It was enough. Nothing, now, could spoil their perfect day.

Back in her bedroom, Karen felt as if she was floating on air. To her knowledge, no-one had seen her come in and she was thankful.

There was a tray beside her bed. On

it was a plate of sandwiches and a flask. Propped up against the flask was a letter. It was from London! It must be from Mr. Arnold.

It vaguely crossed her mind to wonder why it should have been given to her on a Sunday when there was no mail collection. However she slit open the envelope and took out the folded sheet. She read:-

Dear Karen,

Thank you for your very interesting letter, the contents of which have been noted.

It really depends on what Mrs. Hammond has in mind. In the meantime, however, it is up to you to get on with your task quietly and return to London immediately upon completion.

It is best that you do as I ask.

With best wishes,
Jonathan Arnold.

Karen's brow clouded. Mr. Arnold's tone was unmistakable. He wanted her to get on with the cataloguing and waste no time. He made absolutely no reference to the information she had asked for.

She re-read the letter. Knowing her employer as well as she did, she realised that he was trying to tell her something. The phrase '*get on with your task quietly*' was no doubt advising her to say nothing about her discovery of the valuable books. He was asking her to be discreet. That was it . . . and he had not even referred to the conflicting reports concerning Arthur Hammond. Now she understood. He considered that it was none of her business.

She looked again at the envelope. The edges of the flap appeared slightly crinkled. Frances might be right . . . it *could* have been opened before she got it. The delay pointed to that. But she would never know.

"Ho hum," she sighed, leaning back on her pillows. I'll worry about it tomorrow. I'd much rather think about today.

She undressed, showered in her adjoining bathroom, put on her nightgown and climbed into bed.

"Good old Theresa," she whispered aloud, then munched her way through the pile of sandwiches.

Karen had hoped to have breakfast in her room, as usual, but Theresa had brought a message summoning her to the dining room.

To start with, Karen got to the table after everyone else was seated. Laura Hammond's stony silence was, in itself, a rebuke. But there was worse to come.

As Karen unfolded her table napkin, Laura Hammond glared at her. "Miss Warde, I shall be obliged if you will give me an explanation for your absence from *Tabara* yesterday."

Karen jumped. '*Explanation!*' Her mind went into a spin. "But I left you a note on the hall table."

"The note told me nothing. I will repeat my request if you wish. I want an explanation for your inexplicable behaviour."

Karen looked blank.

"You neither informed me where you had gone, nor with whom. I consider your manners more than a little lacking."

Karen felt the blood drain from her face. It had never occurred to her that she had offended the laws of hospitality. She bit her lip. "I'm sorry, Mrs. Hammond.

I guess I didn't think."

"You most certainly did not. I am most displeased. Your behaviour since you have been in my household has been deplorable. I am considering cabling Mr. Arnold to recall you."

"Am I not doing the work to your satisfaction, Mrs. Hammond?"

"Your work is satisfactory, but there are other considerations." She paused, then went on. "You appear to be very dense, Miss Warde. Let me spell it out for you once again. Ever since you have been here I have expressly asked you to refrain from associating with Michael Williamson, and yet you continue to do so, completely disregarding my wishes."

"But all I did was go with him to be with some friends I met on the ship coming over."

"I am quite aware of what you did, Miss Warde, and I will repeat my warning. *If you continue to associate with Michael Williamson you will be asked to leave before completing your assignment.*" Then, shaking with anger, Laura Hammond rose to her feet. "Do I make myself clear?"

Karen nodded dumbly.

"I repeat. If I find that you disobey my wishes just *once* more, you will be sent straight back to London on the first available flight." And with that, she adjusted her chair to its accustomed place and walked out of the room.

There followed an ominous silence, until Warren spoke. "Don't take it too hard. My mother is used to complete obedience."

"But I just don't understand. Why am I not allowed to do as I please on my days off?"

Warren shrugged. "If it were anyone else but Michael Williamson . . . " He left the sentence unfinished, but added, "I can always take you anywhere you want to go."

Karen gave him a baleful look. "And if I do, I suppose I shall get a bruise on the *other* side of my face." She stood up.

Warren looked down at his plate. "I've already apologised for that," he said. "I had had too much champagne. You must have known that. Now, I suppose, I shall never hear the last of it." He stretched out a hand as if to touch her.

She flinched away from him and walked to the door. She was very angry and unhappy. Yesterday had been such a lovely day, and now it was all spoiled.

Warren pushed back his chair and followed her out. "Karen . . . please listen to me . . . " But she walked on towards the library. He followed her, annoyed at her rejection. "Perhaps there will come a time when you need my help . . . and then you will have to ask for it, my high and mighty friend." His tone was threatening.

But Karen muttered to herself, not intending for him to hear, "I shouldn't think *that* very likely." She was fed up with the Hammonds – both of them.

Once in the library she sat down at her desk. She would have to write to Michael and explain the situation. It sounds so stupid for me to have to tell him that I'm not allowed to see him, she thought. It's downright childish. What on earth can I say? And anyway, how can I get a letter to him without Laura Hammond intercepting it? I suppose I'll have to enlist Theresa's help again. She picked up her pen and started to write.

Dear Michael, (how she would love to have written *dearest*)

Mrs. Hammond has taken exception to my association with you, ridiculous though it is. But since I am staying in her house for the time being I have no option but to comply with her wishes.

Please believe me when I say how sorry I am. There is no alternative to doing what she asks of me, since I am here specifically to catalogue the books.

With love, *Karen.*

P.S. Please remember me kindly to Rosemary and her father, and thank you again for Sunday.

She addressed the envelope and sealed it, then put it in her pocket. She would give it to Theresa when she brought in the usual cold drink.

Her thoughts then reverted to the amount of time left to her. At the present rate of progress the work could be finished sooner than she had anticipated. Particularly if she was going to be debarred from pursuing any kind of social life for herself. Her spirits sank when she thought of what she would go back to in London. With no family to welcome her, how could she ever settle down to such a mundane existence again? How *could* she, particularly after experiencing this other world, where the sun always shone and the trees always appeared to be in bloom?

If only her parents were still alive . . . they had been gone just over two years now. She could still feel the pain of that dreadful Saturday morning when they had gone out shopping only to be involved in a car crash and killed outright. She covered her face with her hands, willing herself not to burst into tears.

"Stop feeling so sorry for yourself," she said aloud. "Get on with the job and get out. That's what you've got to do, Karen Warde."

Looking down at her tabulated sheets, she calculated that if she really worked hard it could be done in three more weeks. That estimate meant she would be working the whole time, except for the odd early morning swim or walk in the garden or along the shore. She would also need to work over the two remaining weekends. Yes, she concluded, putting down her pen, I can do it. My deadline shall be the end of May – well, let's say the first of June. I'll do my best to forget everything else for the time being and really concentrate on getting the lists done. Now then, she considered, looking up, which shelf do I tackle next?

She got up, and as she did so, her ball point pen rolled off the desk onto the carpet. She was feeling about under the desk for it when she discovered a slight bump under the carpet, and as she picked up her pen, idly wondered what it could be.

The desk itself was standing on an extra rug which was slightly larger than the area of the desk. Presumably it had been put there to protect the larger one. She dismissed the matter from her mind until later that night when she was in bed. It had excited her curiosity, though she smiled to herself as she was reminded of the fairy story about the princess who could not get comfortable because there was a pea under her mattress.

Her curiosity persisted, and then one

morning, several days later, when Theresa came in with her drink, she found herself asking if the rug was under the desk to protect the carpet.

"No, Miss Karen. Mr. Hammond, he had some fire on the big carpet. That was when he move the desk. He said always to leave the desk on the rug there so it cover the hole."

"I see." she paused, then changed the subject. "Oh, by the way, Theresa, did you manage to get my letter to Mr. Williamson?"

Theresa nodded. "Yessum." She hovered. "Miss Karen, why you aint go out see Mr. Michael no more?"

Karen pushed back her hair to cover her emotion and said, "Mrs. Hammond doesn't wish me to, Theresa."

"But you aint go nowhere."

"No. I have to get the book lists done as quickly as I can and get back to London."

"How does you live there?"

She looked at Theresa intently. "I really don't know how to explain that. It's so different from Bucare."

"And no Mr. Michael, eh?" She grinned.

"Something like that." Karen bent her head to her work.

"Huh, you is some funny woman." And with that cryptic remark, Theresa departed.

Karen's thoughts went back to the rug under the desk. She would not be satisfied until she had discovered what the bump was. But it was not until the end of Harvey's half-term holiday that her chance came.

Harvey went to the Lodge School in Barbados, like his brother before him, and he would not be in Bucare again until the summer holidays. Karen wanted to make sure that she said goodbye to him, for she might never see him again.

As for Harvey, himself, he did not seem at all reluctant to return to school. He came to the library to make a hurried farewell to Karen, saying in a low voice in case he was overheard, "I hope all goes well for you. You're the only one I shall miss — except for Mike, of course."

Karen was sad to see him go. She left the library and went down to watch the pirogue leave the boathouse and set out to sea. Both Laura Hammond and

Warren accompanied him. Harvey waved once and then they were gone. She sighed and went back to the library.

She was sitting and sipping her usual cold drink when she remembered the bump under the carpet. Now was her chance to find out what it was.

First she pushed across the heavy bolt on the inside of the library door to make sure she would not be disturbed. She had no wish to involve Theresa.

The desk was so heavy that though she struggled and struggled to move it, she could not budge it an inch. It felt as if it were screwed to the floor.

Perhaps it would not be so heavy if she took the drawers out first, she thought, and started to remove them. There were four each side, and being soild oak, were very heavy.

When she got to the bottom one on the right, she noticed that there were screws on the casing, set in the direction of the floor. No wonder it had been impossible to budge the desk. It *was* screwed to the floor . . . *and* through two layers of carpet!

She removed the four drawers on the

left and found exactly the same. But without a screwdriver it was impossible to investigate further. She replaced the drawers and considered how best to procure a strong-handled screwdriver. She was sorely tempted to ask Theresa where the tools were kept, but thought better of it. Perhaps there might be some tools in the room over the boathouse. If only she had thought to ask Harvey!

To cover her intention to search the boathouse she changed into her swimsuit and put on a towelling robe. A swim would be a good idea, anyway.

She went down to the boathouse, climbed the steps and opened the door. It was very dim inside. She had noticed before that it had only one small window at the far end.

She felt for the light switch. A hand closed over hers. She gasped. Someone was quietly closing the door with his other hand. Then the light was switched on and she saw who it was.

9

HE held out his arms to her and she almost fell into his embrace. Holding her tight against him, he whispered against her hair, "I have been waiting for you."

"You knew they would be going across to the mainland today?"

"Silly girl. As if I don't know when Harvey is due back at school!"

She moved in his arms. "Of course. I didn't think. You frightened me." A surge of excitement enveloped her. She snuggled up to him, closing her eyes and yielding to the moment. "Oh Michael," she sighed, "it seems so absurd that Mrs. Hammond forbids me to see you."

She looked up at him; in the dim light she could just make out his features. It was at that moment he kissed her, then again when she tried to speak. She forgot what it was she was going to say. He was still holding her close and burying his face in her fragrant hair. "I wanted to see you before I go to Barbados tomorrow," he said.

"That's where Harvey goes to school."

"Yes. My school also. But I'm going for a different reason. I have another plantation over there and it needs a visit now and again. As you know, I've been away for three months, so I must go over and see how things are."

She wanted so much to ask him how long he would be gone.

As if interpreting her silence, he whispered, "I'll be back in a couple of weeks. And whilst I'm gone, don't work too hard."

"I haven't much choice. I want to get this job finished as soon as I can." She paused. "Were you surprised that Mrs. Hammond forbade me to see you?"

"No." He looked unhappy, but held her even closer.

"How did you know I'd come down for a swim?" she whispered.

"I didn't. I was about to enlist Theresa's help to lure you down here."

She sighed contentedly, not wanting him to ever let her go.

Presently, he said, "By the way, your

letter didn't tell me much. How is the job going?"

"Very well. I'm working like mad to finish it as soon as I possibly can."

"When do you think that will be? I should like to be back here before you leave Bucare."

"Well, I've given myself a deadline for the first of June. I want to finish it by then."

"Are you so anxious to leave Bucare?"

"It's not that . . . "

"What, then?"

"Mrs. Hammond can't wait to get rid of me. All she wants from me is to get the cataloguing done and vanish into thin air. It worries me, too, that they appear to be in such a hurry. I have a horrid suspicion that Mrs. Hammond is going to sell the library, complete as it is, and there are some very valuable books in the collection. I'm sure she doesn't realise. And anyway, it seems an awful thing to do."

Michael was thoughtful. "You know, I always expected that Arthur would leave his collection to me."

"Did he ever tell you so?"

"He did, as a matter of fact. I should hate to hear that the collection went out of the family."

"Isn't there anything you can do about it?"

"I don't see what I *can* do." He shrugged then abruptly changed the subject. "What made you come up the stairs?"

Karen thought quickly. "Harvey has taught me how to use flippers. This is where they are kept." She checked herself from adding, 'What I really want is a screwdriver.'

He took her in his arms again. "Dearest Karen," he said, running his fingers up into her hair then holding her face in his hands . . . kissing her just once more, tenderly and with great affection. "I must go now," he said, yet reluctant to release her.

Karen closed her eyes in bliss. She wanted to stay in his arms forever.

At last the moment came for them to part. As he was about to descend the steps at the far end, Karen called, "Michael . . . before you go, would you mind if I asked you a question?" She moved to where he was standing.

"Ask away."

"Why don't you like coming to *Tabara*? There seems to be some mystery about it, but I haven't liked to ask."

His brow clouded, then he said, in very low tones with an unaccustomed twist to his mouth, "My father – my stepfather, that is – drowned with cramp whilst I was busy trimming the sails. We were about to leave the bay where he had spent the day. Arthur had been for a swim and we were just waiting for him to get back on board. As soon as I had set the sails I came back to find Laura and Warren standing at the rail . . . both were watching Arthur struggling in the water. I could hardly believe my eyes. He must have had cramp. I can never believe that they didn't know he was in danger."

Karen caught her breath. "Oh Michael! How awful for you."

He continued. "I dived in when I realised what was happening, but it was too late." He paused, taking a deep breath. "Then they both made a grand production number of helping me bring him up on deck. I did my best to revive him, but it was too late. I suppose the awful struggle he had put up was too much for his heart. He must have wondered why they didn't know he was in difficulties. God! It was a nightmare. I shall never forget it."

Karen could think of nothing to say. Her depth of feeling for what Michael must have suffered gave her pain.

"Now perhaps you can understand why I never come near them," he added, bitterly, turning to descend the steps which led from the far end of the room down into the boathouse itself.

Karen heard him pull the starter cord on the outboard motor of the dinghy and then he was gone. Their parting was, for her, a great wrench.

Though her deep concern for the past filled her thoughts, gradually the memory of his kiss stole upon her senses. Her whole body had responded to his, and the feeling would grow ever stronger, she knew. She still felt the gentle pressure of his lips on hers, and the afterglow of the way he had held her in his arms. A kind of magic coursed through her.

She turned to unlock the door, then remembered about the screwdriver. She found several on a shelf amongst an assortment of tools. She picked one out that looked suitable and took it with her, forgetting all about her intention to swim, and made her way back to the library.

She put the screwdriver in the top drawer of the desk and went to her room to change. For the moment, her curiosity had left her, being replaced by thoughts of Michael. She had discovered that happiness meant being in his arms.

Back in the library her curiosity returned. She took out the screwdriver and considered how best to tackle her problem.

She had pushed back her chair and was about to remove the drawers when she heard a funny scratching noise on the library door. She took no notice at first, thinking it might be Theresa cleaning or dusting, but the scratching developed into a muffled tap.

Hastily replacing the drawers she had already removed, she went to open the door. It was Aunt Hattie.

"Come in, do," said Karen, smiling. "This is a nice surprise."

The old lady looked about her and

then over her shoulder and said, "Where's the boy?"

Karen was puzzled. "He's gone back to school in Barbados, Aunt Hattie. Didn't he say goodbye to you? Or have you forgotten?"

"No, I haven't forgotten. I don't mean that one. I mean Michael." Aunt Hattie put her finger to her lips and cast an anxious look behind her. "He's my God-son, you know. But we mustn't say his name. She won't like it."

"Please come in," said Karen, kindly, putting an arm around Aunt Hattie's shoulders. "Theresa is just about to bring in my drink. Would you like some coffee? I'll ask her to make you some."

When Karen returned, the old lady was sitting at the desk. She looked up and smiled tremulously. "They've gone to Barbados, haven't they?"

Karen nodded. "To take Harvey back to school."

"They don't know everything I know," continued Aunt Hattie. "I never talk to them."

Karen was non-plussed. She wanted very much to converse with Aunt Hattie, but it was so difficult to know what to say to her because it was impossible to follow her thoughts.

Theresa brought in the tray and laid it on the desk. She hesitated. "Would she like some of she medicine? Just a smidgin?"

Aunt Hattie's eyes grew bright. She nodded vigorously.

Theresa returned with a tot of whisky. Aunt Hattie snatched at it and tipped it into her coffee cup, motioning Karen to fill it up from the coffee pot and imperiously handing back the empty glass to Theresa. "You're a good girl, Theresa," she said. "A very kind girl."

Theresa gave Karen a surreptitious wink as she went out.

Aunt Hattie seemed to come to life and grew more coherent under the influence of the alcohol. It was clearly a treat which she was seldom allowed. She sat back, a happy languor overcoming her. She looked up at Karen, who was standing beside her. "You're not one of the family, are you?"

"No. Aunt Hattie. I'm not one of the family," repeated Karen.

"Then what are you doing here?"

"I'm here to catalogue the books."

"Oh yes, I remember now." She slipped her laced coffee with appreciation. "My boy would like you, though," she added.

Karen waited.

"This is *his* room, you know," the old lady went on. "I know that, but *they* don't." She turned her face towards the door. "Are they coming yet?"

"No. Not yet."

"They don't like me coming in here. They *never* let me come in here."

"Why ever not?"

"I don't know." She drank the last of her coffee and shakily replaced the cup on its saucer, onesidedly. "Yes, I do know why," she added, quietly. "They think I know where the will is and they don't want me to find it. I *did* know, but I can't remember any more. Arthur told me. It's somewhere in this room."

"A will? You mean . . . a will is lost?"

Aunt Hattie was star-gazing now, but she went on, "Even if I did remember I wouldn't tell them. I don't like being badgered. I don't like it." Suddenly she sat up, giving Karen a piercing look. "*You* know my boy, don't you!"

"Yes, Aunt Hattie, I do. I met him on the ship coming over."

"So he's back again." She mused over this information then asked. "Will he come to see me, do you think?"

But Karen was at a loss to know what to reply.

"To know him is to love him, eh?"

Karen glanced at the tray, embarrassment flooding her at the realisation that she did, indeed, love Michael.

Mercifully the old lady said nothing more. By now the whisky was beginning to wear off and she reverted to her usual vague state. Karen helped her up from the chair. She was unsteady on her feet but refused assistance. Karen opened the door for her then sat down at the desk once more. Her heart was light. The old lady's final remark had started a small song somewhere inside her head, and the chorus repeated itself over and over . . . '*To know him is to love him*' it went.

She tried to get her mind back to her work, but found great difficulty in concentrating. The ball point pen she was using gave out. Impatient, she opened the desk drawer to search for another and the screwdriver rolled forward. She picked it up. The temptation and the diversion was too great to resist. She just had to discover what the bump was.

Once again she removed the drawers, then kneeling down, sat back on her heels contemplating the screws.

I think I had better lock the door, again, she told herself.

When she had done so she got down again and managed to dislodge the first screw, then the second and third. There were eight in all. It was hard work – they had rusted from not having been moved for some years.

The desk was heavy, and it took her some time to move it across on to the large carpet. When she managed that she pulled back the top rug. Yes, there was certainly a large patch of burnt carpet beneath it. An area of about a square metre had been destroyed.

Then she saw a brass catch-ring which protruded from an oblong panel set into the parquet flooring. She slipped her finger into the catch and lifted it still further. She pulled it even harder and the oblong panel came with it. Underneath was a small compartment, asbestos lined, containing documents. Her curiosity never even stopped her from taking them out.

Amongst the various papers was a document that was obviously a will. Yes, it was quite obviously a will.

With shaking fingers she opened it up and started to read it. There was one thing she was looking for and that was reference to the library. So, this was the document that Aunt Hattie had rambled on about.

Karen knew she had no business to read the will, but something drove her on. Was there any reference to the books? She had to know.

At last she found it — on the third page at the bottom. Clearly and unequivocably the library had been willed to Michael. That was all she wanted to know.

She replaced all the documents, including an envelope addressed to someone called *de Freitas*, as carefully as she could. Nothing must look as it if had been tampered with.

Hurriedly she replaced the lid, pressed the catch ring down into its socket and pulled the carpet back in place. Dragging the desk back to its original position was very difficult, and getting the screws into position even worse, and all the time her heart thumped away with apprehension for what she had done. By the time she had put everything back in its place she was completely exhausted.

Now what am I supposed to do? I must prevent Michael's library from being sold.

She knew there was nobody she could turn to at *Tabara*, and now Michael had gone away. She would just have to go and see Frances about it. Perhaps she could advise her. No time must be wasted, since the book list was almost finished.

She unlocked the door and opened it. There were voices coming from the kitchen. Laura Hammond must have returned already. She breathed a sigh of relief that she had put the desk back in the nick of time.

Tomorrow was Friday. Saturday was her day off. She could go across to the mainland and see Frances.

That evening at suppertime Karen told Laura Hammond that she would like to visit Trinidad on Saturday, but she said nothing about visiting friends.

"Warren will be pleased to take you across. He will be collecting supplies, as usual."

"I . . . ," began Karen, again wishing she could have asked Winston to take her. However, she changed her mind. Everything must appear casual. "Thanks," she said, looking down at her plate.

The next morning they left the boathouse at nine o'clock, and Warren was at his friendly best. He was attentive yet impersonal, yet Karen could never trust him again.

He waited until they were on the quayside before he asked her where she was going.

"To do some shopping. I want to get one or two souvenirs to take back to England with me." She would have to be doubly careful not to reveal her intention to visit Frances, even though she had no idea of her whereabouts. She had her address, and with luck the cab driver would know where *La Fantasie* was.

Warren hailed a cab and got in beside her. She was annoyed, but said nothing.

"Frederick Street?" he questioned her.

She nodded. By now she had gathered that Warren was not to be shaken off so easily.

"What time would you like me to be back on the quayside?" she asked him, as innocently as she could.

"Oh, I'll come with you. I can show you where the best bargains are. And later, perhaps, we can have lunch together."

Karen squirmed. "I should much prefer to have a free day – by *myself*," she said, firmly.

He was annoyed.

"Well, perhaps we might have a drink together, later," she tempered. "I could meet you at the Angostura bar, like last time."

"But I may as well come with you. I haven't anything better to do."

Oh dear, wailed Karen, inwardly. Is there no shaking him off? "Please don't think me ungracious, Warren, but I *really should* prefer to be alone. I'm sorry."

He was clearly piqued. "Very well. I'll see you at four o'clock."

"Where?"

"In the restaurant of the Emporium."

She nodded and sighed with relief.

The cab stopped and they got out.

Karen stared after him, watching to see where he went. She saw him hurrying into the Bombay Bazaar, but nevertheless sensed that he intended to follow her anyway.

She had guessed correctly. She walked into the nearest large department store and entered the lift just in time to see him come in after her.

As the lift doors closed he made for the stairs, but Karen was not intending to be outdone this time. She pressed the button for the fourth floor, then pressed it again when it reached the top, remaining in the lift and travelling down to ground level again.

She rushed out of the store and hailed a cab. It took only seconds for her to jump in and give the driver Frances's address.

"Please hurry," she said.

The cab river knew exactly where La Fantasie was. They drove round the Savannah and past the Botanical Gardens then left into a quiet *cul-de-sac.*

The driver slowed and craned his neck to make sure he had the right house, then carefully eased the cab into the driveway of a soft dark pink house of Spanish design.

As Karen paid off the cab and climbed out, a louvre above opened and was folded back. She watched the hands. They undoubtedly belonged to Frances. Then her head appeared. She did not even look surprised to see Karen.

"You're too late for breakfast," she quipped.

Karen found herself giggling. She had really enjoyed giving Warren the slip.

Within seconds she was ushered in and served with a cold drink.

"And what can we do for *you*?" Frances grinned.

Karen swallowed hard. "I hardly know where to begin."

"Where we left off, I should imagine."

Karen told her everything, and Frances listened intently.

After a few seconds thought, Frances said, "I think we had better get Giles here." She picked up the telephone and dialled. After a brief conversation Frances said, "He'll be home in a few minutes. Luckily he's working at the Botanical Gardens today. That's just around the corner. Perhaps you noticed it as you came by."

Karen nodded.

"You'll have lunch with us, of course."

"That would be lovely."

"What's this all about?" asked Giles as he strolled in.

"Tell him, Karrie."

Karen repeated her story, including her discovery of the cache of documents.

Giles looked serious. "After considering the facts," he said, "I honestly don't think you can do much about it, Karen. Except tell Michael, that is. He will have to decide, himself, how to tackle the situation." He paused. "I think you must be very careful not to admit that you yourself have any knowledge of the contents of the will. Laura Hammond might make life very unpleasant for you, if you do."

"Yes," admitted Karen. "I know it was wrong of me to pry, really, but I can't bear the thought of that wonderful collection of books being disposed of."

IOB17

"In the circumstances it's lucky you *did* do some poking around," put in Frances.

"Actually, I feel terrible now that I realise what I've done . . . " she paused. "What ever Michael will think of me I dare not guess!"

Giles asked, "When you were sorting through the documents under the floor, did you notice whether any solicitor's name was mentioned?"

"Yes. Someone called Da Freitas, I believe."

"That would be it. Da Freitas – Louis da Freitas – it's an old established firm in Barbados. They are the people to get in touch with. But not by us. By Michael."

Frances said, "But surely Laura Hammond would have got in touch with them when her husband died."

"Perhaps she didn't. Perhaps she didn't know about the will. In any case, Louis de Freitas would have a copy."

"I remember now," said Karen. "There was an *envelope* addressed to Louis de Freitas."

"Then the solicitors cannot know that

Arthur Hammond is dead," said Karen. "Perhaps Laura Hammond didn't even know about the will."

"I suppose it's possible," agreed Giles. "But unlikely, surely."

"But that would mean that Arthur Hammond didn't trust his wife," added Frances.

Karen interposed. "Harvey, Michael's young brother, indicated that his step-father was disenchanted with Laura Hammond some time before he died."

Giles stood up. "I must get back to the Gardens. Leave it with me, Karen. I'll see that Michael gets all the information. You say he's in Barbados? In that case I'll get a message to him, then he can go and see Da Freitas himself. Don't worry." He paused. "And don't worry too much about the prying. The library might easily have been disposed of if you hadn't done what you did."

Frances and Karen had a light lunch together and then it was time for Karen to be at her rendezvous with Warren. She knew that he would be furious with her for giving him the slip, but by now she did not even care. Soon the books would all be listed and she could be done with the whole thing.

Frances drove her back to Frederick Street and dropped her outside the Emporium. She got into the lift and went to the top floor restaurant to see Warren slumped at a table. He was clearly in a sulk.

She sat down at his table and the waitress came across to take their order. When she had gone, he snarled, “I suppose you think you are pretty clever.”

“You asked for it. I tried to tell you that I wanted to be on my own.”

“Where have you been?”

Karen did not answer, and there was no conversation between them for the remainder of the day.

10

BY four o'clock on the afternoon of the thirtieth of May, Karen had come to the end of her task. She had a feeling of satisfaction for the job accomplished, but she had a growing fear of the showdown which would be inevitable between Laura Hammond and Michael, and she began to dread Laura Hammond's wrath when she discovered that she, Karen, had been the person to discover the will. She prayed that she could get away from *Tabara* before the fireworks started.

By now Giles would have contacted Michael, and no doubt Michael had called on the solicitor (da Freitas) in Barbados and told him of Arthur Hammond's death. It was perhaps amazing that the solicitor had not already heard about it, for news travels fast in the West Indies, or anywhere, for that matter.

Karen devoutly hoped that Laura Hammond could be restrained from disposing of the library, now rightfully Michael's, before it was too late. She wondered again whether Michael had yet been to see the Solicitor. All she could do was wait and see. Although she kept telling herself it was none of her business she felt personally involved because of what she had done in discovering the floor safe.

There was at least something she could do, and that was to send Michael word, as she had promised him, that her job was now completed. Her letter would be waiting for him when he returned from Barbados.

> '*Dear Michael,*' she wrote. '*It's done. I am leaving here tomorrow. I shall ask Warren to take me to Trinidad so that I can stay with Frances until my plane leaves. Au revoir – I'll never forget you. Love, Karen.*'

The last sentence was as daring as she could make it in the present circumstances. She would hand the finished sheaf of papers to Laura Hammond at supper time that evening and then do her packing. She did not wish to stay at *Tabara* a moment longer than was necessary.

Karen held the note in her hand as she left the library and walked along to the kitchen to give it to Theresa, but Laura Hammond was there, and she had not expected her to be.

She hastily thrust the letter into her pocket when she saw Laura Hammond, but she was not quick enough.

"Is that a letter you want posted, Miss Warde?"

"It can wait. It — it's not important." Karen was vaguely aware that Theresa had walked out of the kitchen, no doubt terrified of being involved or perhaps guessing at Karen's intention.

"Surely it must be. You were obviously in a great hurry." She held out her hand to take the letter, but Karen backed away. She was suddenly frightened.

Warren came up behind her. "Take it from her," Laura Hammond said, icily.

"But it is *my* letter," protested Karen.

Laura Hammond continued to point and Warren aggressively caught hold of Karen's arm in a vice-like grip. She struggled, but he was too strong for her and manhandled her until he had the letter in his hand. He gave it to his mother and she read the name on the envelope.

"So," she said, menacingly, "you are still disobeying my orders." Her eyes narrowed to slits.

"No. Mrs. Hammond . . . I am *not* . . . I only wanted to let Michael know that I have finished my job here because I promised him I would. I have the lists ready for you . . . I was going to give them to you at suppertime. All I want to do is let Michael know that I *have* finished what I came to do . . . because he asked me to." Angry tears sprang to her eyes.

"You will do nothing of the kind."

"But surely you have no right to interfere with me like this!" Her voice weakened in desperation.

"I have every right. Whilst you are in my house you will do as I say. And I'd like the completed work now, if you please."

Karen, indignant, and feeling very much wronged, reluctantly made her way to the library with Laura Hammond and

Warren following her.

Karen went over to the desk to pick up the thick sheaf of papers she had left there only minutes ago, but they had vanished.

"They've gone!" she gasped. "Someone must have taken them." She searched frantically, also in each drawer, but there was no sign of them.

"Well," said Laura Hammond, quiet as marble, "Where are they?"

"I just don't know." Karen stood there helplessly. She felt desolate, thinking of all the hard work she had put in. "They *must* be *somewhere*," she went on, stalling for time. She was nonplussed. "I really cannot understand what has happened," she added, lamely.

"Then you had better soon remember what you *have* done with them." Laura Hammond was enraged. "You have been in my house for over two months. You won't get away with this."

"B-but I have worked so hard on them. Why would anyone want to take them?"

"That is what I should like to know. I had arranged for the whole library to be collected and shipped to the U.S.A.

as soon as the cataloguing was finished. Now what am I going to do?"

"But you *can't* do that!" Karen burst out. "You just *can't*."

Laura Hammond frowned. "What on earth are you talking about?"

"The books are not yours to dispose of," went on Karen, quite recklessly. She could not seem to stop herself – caution had gone to the winds.

Instead of replying, Laura Hammond turned to Warren. "Take her to her room and see that she stays there."

Warren caught Karen by the shoulder and twisted her arm right behind her back. The pain of it made her cry out. "No! *Please*. I'll go quietly."

Warren released her, but his face still registered malicious intent. He punched her in the back and it almost winded her. Oh, what a stupid thing I have done, she wailed inwardly. Whatever made me blurt out about the books not belonging? I suppose I'm getting all I've asked for, floated through her mind, even in her panic. What ever will they do to me?

As she struggled up the stairs with Warren continually thumping her she sensed he was really enjoying himself and getting back at her for her continued rejection of him.

It was with some relief that she at last reached her bedroom. He flung open the door, pushed her roughly inside and turned the key on the outside.

Karen threw herself on the bed and beat her fists into the pillows. She was absolutely furious. Not only with Laura Hammond and her son Warren, but with herself, as she thought of all the trouble she might now have caused. Mr. Arnold had cautioned her and both Frances and Giles had warned her to be careful not to divulge what she knew, yet she had stupidly blurted it out.

Laura Hammond was bound to speculate on where her information came from, and suspicion might very well rest on poor Aunt Hattie. They would be bound to have heard Aunt Hattie make her accusation more than once. Luckily the old lady knew nothing about the location of the will, so they would be unable to discover where it was, but they might well bully the poor old soul. Oh dear! If she, Karen, were questioned, she would just have to tell them. But what *could* she tell them? That she had snooped about under the desk and even gone so far as to almost dismantle it in her avid curiosity? She pressed her hands to her temples in an effort to think straight, then sat up, laconically dangling her legs over the edge of the bed. *What on earth could she do?*

The house was now completely silent and she guessed the family were in the dining room.

About nine o'clock she heard approaching footsteps. They were unmistakably Laura Hammond's. Then she heard several other pairs of feet, including Theresa's. They stopped at her door. The key turned and Laura Hammond and Warren entered, followed by Theresa, looking very unhappy and bearing a tray of supper.

"Put the tray on the table and go," Laura Hammond instructed Theresa. Then turning to Warren, she said, sarcastically, "We cannot allow our guests to starve."

Karen said nothing.

"Now," said Laura Hammond. "I want to know where you got the idea that the library of books downstairs is not mine. I insist you tell me."

"No, I refuse."

Warren looked questioningly at his mother. "You want me to try persuasion?"

"Not yet. We will leave her to cool off a little as a first resort. Leave the room, Warren." She waited until he had left and then spoke once more in the icy tone Karen had come to expect from her. "There are two things I want, young woman. One is the completed catalogue you have been working on for the past two and a half months, and the other . . . *I want to know where your information concerning the ownership of the library came from.*"

Karen sat on the edge of the bed in silence, and the longer she said nothing the angrier Laura Hammond grew. "Well, my girl," she said, "We'll give you another twenty-four hours. After that it will be the worse for you," she threatened. Then she stalked out and the door was slammed and locked once again.

Karen glanced at the tray. There was a tolerable cold supper laid out, but she had no appetite. She decided she might as well try to get some sleep. But she would not undress. Anything might happen. Perhaps she'd be thrown to the sharks!

The hours went slowly by and eventually the sounds in the household died down and she guessed that everyone had gone to bed.

She woke at midnight, very hungry. She pulled the tray across onto the bed and started to eat.

She had just bitten into a roll when she heard the key turn in the lock. Her blood ran cold. It was probably Warren.

The handle turned and the door opened. Karen felt the blood leave her head and her scalp went all prickly. She tried to put the tray back onto the side-table but her hands were shaking so much that it slithered across the bed and crashed onto the floor.

The door closed again, the key was turned and all was quiet again. She had been lucky this time! But she knew she would never be able to get to sleep.

At about three in the morning she heard the key turn again. Once more the handle turned and the door opened, very slowly.

She slid quietly out of bed in the dark and crawled underneath it. Her face came into contact with an up-turned fork which had fallen off the tray when it slipped. She grabbed it eagerly. It might serve as a weapon.

She waited. There was no sound at first, though she was certain that someone was in the room. She peered into the gloom. Perhaps she could see Warren's feet, but no — and then the light was switched on and she could see two bunches of pink feathers. Slippers! It must be Aunt Hattie, for she could not imagine Laura Hammond wearing anything so frivolous.

A face appeared, upside down. It *was* Aunt Hattie. "Oh, there you are, dear," she said, "I always think that under the bed is a good place to be if you aren't sure."

Karen crawled out of her hiding place and put a finger to her lips. "Ssh . . . if they find you here there will be awful trouble."

"I'm not staying, my dear. I only came to tell you that *I've* got the papers. I'm keeping them safe for you."

"Oh, Aunt Hattie! What a relief. That

was so kind of you, but you shouldn't have done it. Let me have them back, please. I want to leave and they won't let me out of my room until I've handed them over."

"But I don't want them to get Michael's books."

"They won't. You'll see. Michael will think of a way. Please, *please* let me have them. I must give them to Mrs. Hammond."

By now Karen was in a state of anxiety. She was desperately afraid that Aunt Hattie might destroy the lists. She waited patiently, but the old lady was not at all anxious to co-operate. Finally, however, she relented and said, "Oh, all right. I'll have to trust you, I suppose." She hesitated. "You want me to go and get them? Now?"

"No. Don't do that. Please . . . put them back on the desk in the library tomorrow – exactly where you got them from."

"*Must* I?"

Karen nodded. "Remember. Not now. In the morning. Do you promise?"

"Very well, dear."

"And don't worry. Michael will think of a way. You wait and see." She led her to the door. "Ssh," she cautioned, as she gently turned the handle.

Karen opened the door and looked up and down the passage. A dim light was kept on all night. "It's all clear," she whispered, and as Aunt Hattie departed Karen withdrew the key from the lock and turned it on the inside. Now is my chance, she decided.

She went to the wardrobe and collected her coat, then picked up her purse and put it in her pocket. She would leave the house; it was the only thing to do. But what if they caught her? She refused to listen to her fears. All she wanted to do was get away and she did not much care how she did it. Swim, if necessary!

Carefully she made her way to the side door. Mercifully it was unlocked, as usual. She slid out quietly and melted into the night. But where could she go? And she had no means of getting anywhere, anyway.

Then a thought came to her. What about the pirogue? No, that would be impossible . . . or *would* it?

She tiptoed down to the boathouse. The door was closed. Locked. Perhaps she could get in through the upstairs room that by now she knew so well.

She ran hurriedly up the steps and tried the door. It was open. She locked it behind her. That ought to give her a good start.

The steps down into the boathouse proper were dark and she stumbled several times. Her legs were shaking and her heart beating so fast she thought it would burst.

It was eerie in the boathouse below. The water lapped and gleamed intermittently from the light of the now waning moon. She could see the pirogue, dimly silhouetted. But then she realised it would be suicidal to start up the engine inside the boathouse. The sound would reverberate ten-fold and Warren would sprint down there in no time.

She looked around the wall but could see very little, and she dare not turn on the light. Perhaps if she felt along the walls there might be something she could use – a pole or something to push the pirogue away from the inside of the boathouse.

Her hands came into contact with an oar. In fact there were two. She struggled to lift them off their hooks, almost overbalancing in her efforts, as the platform at the sides of the boathouse was very narrow and the planking unsteady.

At last she got them free and carefully let them down into the pirogue. They were impossibly heavy. Her intention was to get some way out to sea and then make an effort to start up the engine. But everything she tried to do proved much harder than she anticipated.

Firstly, being entirely ignorant of boats, she discovered she was vainly trying to row in an opposite direction to that in which she intended to go, and after sorting that out, found the boat would not budge until she discovered the reason. It was still tied up. In her panic she had completely overlooked the fact.

The rope was coarse and her fingers sore by the time she had managed to loosen the knot. Why did it have to be so difficult? Warren always did it easily enough.

Eventually the pirogue began to move, ponderously at first, and fortune was with her at last – up to a point. The tide was on the turn – going out – and she was able to capitalise on this. A sense of exhilaration filled her as the boat got further and further from the boathouse.

But the pirogue was a heavy, cumbersome craft, and she quickly wearied. So terribly, terribly weary, and in the end she was so exhausted from struggling to use the oars efficiently that she had to give up and drift.

She went hopefully to the controls. It was at that moment she realised the enormity of what she had done. The key was not in the ignition, and without it she had no hope of starting the engine. Not only that, she realised that she was guilty of theft. There was nothing she could do but sit it out in the hope that someone would rescue her.

Daylight seemed a century away.

11

THE remainder of the night had not been uncomfortably cold, just chilly. Karen had closed the sliding door before lying down with her coat over her. But she got thirsty, and like the ancient mariner, there was 'nor any drop to drink'.

The hopelessness of her situation bore down upon her, and her mind was numbed with worry over what she had done. Over and over she reproached herself for taking the pirogue, but over and over again she told herself that there had been no alternative. She had been frightened – really frightened – for the first time in her life.

Her thoughts, as ever, kept turning to Michael. How he would despise her weakness. She deserved nothing more than contempt for blurting out what she knew to be the truth. He would never forgive her for that. He *couldn't*!

Then there was poor Aunt Hattie who

had tried to help her. She also was probably in deep trouble by now. What would the Hammonds do to her when they found out that not only had she taken the catalogue but that she had unlocked Karen's door so that she could escape? Or if she had hidden the papers again, as well she might, who could tell whether she would forget where she had hidden them? Anxieties came crowding in on her and she slept only fitfully.

With the dawn, Karen awoke to find the windows of the cabin opaque. Panic clutched her until she realised that the boat was shrouded in mist. The silence, too, was eerie. Not even a cry from a seagull, and the sea a dead calm. She wanted to scream. It was surely a nightmare.

She opened the sliding door to discover that the mist was already lifting off the sea. A pale sunlight penetrated the atmosphere giving everything an unearthly greenish glow. Beneath the boat the water showed crystal clear, impenetrably deep yet all life below the surface suffused in the weird light from the lambent sun.

Karen returned to the cabin. The mist still clung to the windows, but she was reassured knowing that soon, very soon now, the mist would clear and the sun would come through in all its tropical splendour.

She put on her coat, which she had used as a covering during the night, and sat down on the bench, disconsolately. If only I could find something to drink, she lamented. I am so terribly thirsty. Perhaps a systematic search of the boat might reveal a spare tin of beer or something.

The cupboards were full of a variety of things but not a drop of anything to drink . . . nor eat . . . for that matter. She then explored the stern, which took up half the length of the pirogue. Pieces of sacking and empty fish baskets there were in plenty, but little else besides a gaff and a coil of thick rope.

She wandered back to the cabin and sat down again, swinging her legs for want of something better to do. Her heels came back on something less rigid than wood. She got down and peered under the seat and could see a large cardboard carton. Was it too much to hope that there was something edible in it?

She tugged at it. It was wedged in between two stays. She struggled until it was free and pulled it out and lifted the flap. What a find! The carton contained about two dozen tins of processed peas.

She speculated on what they were doing there. To her knowledge, she had never remembered having been served processed peas at *Tabara*. Perhaps they had been accidentally included in supplies at some time. Anyhow, she could not worry about that now. Steal some or not, she was desperate for something to drink, and the liquid the peas were tinned in would satisfy her for the time being. Maybe even a few peas would not come amiss. Tinned peas for breakfast! It might set a fashion.

A bait knife. Where did she see one? Ah, in the small compartment by the wheel. She grabbed it and wiped it on a tissue from her coat pocket and set about opening one of the tins.

Soon she was back on the seat swinging her legs again, this time triumphantly holding a jaggedly opened tin of peas in one hand, and with the other was dipping her fingers into the contents and eating them with relish. Now and then she took a careful sip of the liquid so as not to cut her lips; it was slightly salty, but far less than sea water. They tasted wonderful!

The morning wore on, but nothing happened except now and then a seagull perched on the side of the boat, then rose into the blue above, its cries mocking her distress.

It was hot now. She scanned the sea. There was no sign of land and no hint of another boat. It was ominous, to say the least. Her spirits sank lower and lower.

What made things even worse was that she had no sense of time. All she could go by was the row of three now empty tins on the seat beside her. Her watch had stopped because she had forgotten to wind it the night before. There was absolutely nothing she could do except hope that someone would see her and rescue her from her plight. She was drifting further and further out to sea, away from the island and away from Trinidad.

It was almost noon now, from the position of the sun, and the cabin was stifling. She pulled a seat cushion outside into the stern and sat with a piece of sacking over her head to shield her face from the sun, then dozed off.

The sound of an outboard motor woke her. She shook herself to make sure she was not dreaming then sat up, alert now. A small fishing boat with an outboard motor was heading towards the pirogue. As it got nearer she recognised who was at the tiller.

"Winston! Winston!" She stood up, waving both arms frantically.

"Hold on, Miss Karen. I coming," he called.

She could not quite believe that her nightmare was over. It was a wonderful relief to see Winston when it might so easily have been Warren Grant.

"I comin' to get you," he called, manoeuvering alongside.

"No, no, no! *Please* no! Take me *anywhere* please Winston, but not *Tabara.*"

Winston held up his hand. "Wait! I must tie the boat first." He busied himself with the task of using the coil of rope to tie his own boat to the stern of the pirogue, then jumped board.

"*Please* don't take me back to *Tabara*," Karen pleaded, once again.

"Don't worry. I aint intend taking you back there. But Mistress Hammond she plenty mad at you. Warren, he want to take my boat from me to come and get you, but Theresa, she say not to let him have it."

"Oh, what can I do, Winston? Whatever can I do?" Karen clasped and unclasped her hands agitatedly.

"Should I take you to Mr. Michael?"

"No, no, no. Anyway, he's in Barbados."

"What about Mistress Drake, then?"

"Yes. That would be best. Could you take me over to Trinidad?"

Winston nodded. "We go Trinidad first, then I take the pirogue back to *Tabara*." He went forward into the cabin and bent down to floor level. Karen wondered what he was doing. When he got up he held up a small black box the size of a matchbox. Karen looked at him, puzzled.

"The spare," he said, grinning at her as he slid back the lid and took out a key which he inserted into ignition.

"How did you know it was there?"

There was no reply except a knowing

smile as he turned the key and the engine sprang to life.

"You've done this before," said Karen. "I wish I had known."

Winston nodded, then glanced back over his shoulder to reassure himself that his own boat was correctly positioned for towing.

And then they were moving. Thank heaven for Winston! It would have been a different story if Warren Grant had caught up with her. She shuddered to think what would have come later.

Karen kept silent until her tension had lessened and the coast of Trinidad was visible. Apparently she had not drifted as far as she imagined. She now felt concern for the part Winston had played.

"When you get back to *Tabara* and I'm not with you, will they be angry with you, Winston?"

"Yes, but I'll not see them. Just put the pirogue in the boathouse and leave quick quick." He grinned.

"I just don't know how to thank you. What would have happened to me if you hadn't found me, I dare not imagine!"

"Theresa tell me to come look for you."

"Will she get into trouble for helping me?"

"She already leave. She gone to she home at Arima."

"And Tracy?"

"Uhuh."

"Oh dear!"

"No worry. Theresa can always find new work. She good good."

"Yes, Winston. I know she is. Very good."

They were nearing Trinidad. The harbour wall was in sight. Karen had a familiar feeling as she waited for Winston to secure the pirogue.

She followed him up the steps on to the quay and her fears left her. She was safe in Trinidad. Though England was several thousand miles away it was within reach now. Just a plane trip and she could be there.

But first she had to see Frances. Her mind was still in a whirl and she had no idea what her best course of action should be. She still felt badly at having stolen the pirogue and because of it felt a decided disinclination to face Michael, certain in her mind that he would be severely disappointed in her behaviour.

A cab drew up almost immediately, just as it had happened twice before. Winston opened the cab door for her and she thanked him once again. Then Winston and the cab driver struck up a hearty exchange which lasted some time.

When they finally drove off, Karen said, "La Fantasie, please," and the cab driver raised his hand in acknowledgement.

As the vehicle gained momentum Karen wondered whether Frances would be annoyed with her. She felt desperate, but she *had* to get away from *Tabara.* It would have been impossible to stay there any longer.

Karen sipped the welcome hot milk and endeavoured to relate all that had happened.

"Honestly, you *are* an idiot," commented Frances. "Why on earth didn't you stand up to them?"

"It's all very well for *you* to talk," she replied, dispiritedly, "but you don't know what they're like. I was scared to death."

"Looks as if you aren't much good at

taking care of yourself."

"Oh, don't say that, Frances. You make me feel such a wash-out."

"Well, *you* said it, I didn't," returned Frances.

Karen took another sip of her hot milk and said, "You're quite right. I've made a stupid mess of *everything*."

"Don't be a loon. I don't suppose I would really have done any different in your situation. Those two sound as if they are a pretty formidable team."

By now Karen's confusion was beginning to wear off, but she was mentally and physically exhausted. Frances was observant enough to see that she was almost at the end of her tether.

"You had better go to bed. I'll put you in the guest room. We'll talk tomorrow." Frances took her into a cool darkened room without air-conditioning. Karen undressed and put on a borrowed nightgown and sank gratefully into bed. Oblivion was what she craved. She could not think straight and her eyelids had begun to droop.

"Have a good sleep, Karrie. Forget about everything until the morning."

Frances walked towards the door and turned. "By the way, I forgot to ask if you were hungry."

"I could have been, but I'm too weary to eat at the moment."

"Did you find anything to eat on the boat? An odd shrimp or two, maybe?"

Karen managed a feeble grin. "A crate of tinned peas. I ate three whole tins." She turned over on her side and closed her eyes, but she could hear Frances laughing all the way down the passage.

Being in a comfortable bed was bliss. The sheets smelled of something clean and delicious and indefinable, though she could not get to sleep for a long time.

Going over the events of her stay on Bucare, she was particularly dismayed at the realisation that she had let Mr. Arnold down. The thought oppressed her and she knew she must get back to London and explain to him all that had happened. She would have to hope that he understood how difficult it had been. She had been so proud to be trusted to come out to the West Indies and do the cataloguing, and yet so much had gone wrong.

What *made* things so wrong, she asked

herself. The answer came back loud and clear. You fell in love with Michael Williamson – that's what went wrong. That's the cause of all the trouble. If you had never met Michael, everything would have been all right.

Oh, Michael, Michael . . . she struggled restlessly until at last she fell into a deep sleep.

The following morning Frances woke her with a tray of tea and sat on the end of the bed watching her. "Feel better?" she asked.

Karen nodded. "Amazingly."

"What would you like to do today?"

"Get on a plane for London," said Karen, without hesitation.

"You *aren't* going back to England before you have seen Michael, surely!" Frances was aghast.

"I'm sorry, Frances, but I've made up my mind. I just can't face him again after what I've done."

Frances wagged her head in disbelief.

Two hours later, accompanied by Frances, Karen picked up her ticket from the information desk.

Frances was very quiet and Karen knew that she was impatient with her, but she could think of nothing to say.

Everything happened very quickly. The flight was called and Karen, overcome, gave Frances a quick hug and a tearful kiss then walked towards the flight number exit.

Frances ran after her and said, irritably, "Oh Karrie, why don't you grow up? Michael is going to be so upset when he finds you have gone back to England."

Karen flushed but continued walking to the flight exit. At the gate she turned to smile and wave, but Frances had gone. So much for this whole episode, thought Karen. Thank goodness it's over.

But sitting back in her seat on the aircraft and looking down at the aquamarine and silver sea, she felt that part of her had been left behind. She would be for ever longing to be back on the deck of the '*Ibis*' by Michael's side and watching the scarlet sails fill with the exhilarating trade winds.

She gave a deep sigh and dragged her eyes away from the window. It was more than she could do to forget . . . ever.

At Heathrow Airport Karen felt very lonely. As she walked through the Customs Hall she was reminded that she did not even have any baggage to collect. What little she had taken with her remainded at *Tabara.* She had the sensation that she was shrinking.

She glanced towards the conveyor belt where passengers awaited their personal luggage to come riding through the aperture and round on the carousel. It had never struck her before how like parcels people became when they travelled by air. A kind of paralysis was written on the faces of her fellow travellers and yet, as soon as they left the Customs Hall with their belongings and proceeded to the exit where friends and relatives were gathered at the barrier to greet them, their faces became animated once more, just as if they had emerged from a long dark tunnel.

Karen watched enviously as people were greeted by their loved ones. There was no-one to meet her. How could there be? The detachment of her situation depressed her. All she really wanted to do was run back to Michael — to be in his arms once again – to feel his kisses. She closed her eyes, trying to imagine he was beside her, his masculinity affording her the protection she now craved. It was something she had never known before she had met him. Vulnerability yes, but never love, except from her parents. And now, having fallen in love, she would forever be aware of that indefinable yearning that comes to a woman when her whole being seeks to be with the man she loves.

"Don't be dotty," she told herself, aloud. It was merely an infatuation. What an absurd situation. She could almost hear Frances saying, 'You'll just have to come down to earth again, my girl.'

12

A WEEK had passed, and Karen had done her best to settle back into her old routine at the bookshop. Her landlady had welcomed her and Karen was grateful for her kindness since she was feeling very much alone.

Mr. Arnold had greeted her in a fatherly way. His manner was indulgent and in no way did he let her feel she had let him down.

On that first morning back at the bookshop Karen had related everything that had happened on Bucare, and her employer listened attentively.

"I'm so sorry that there was trouble, Mr. Arnold, but Mrs. Hammond was dead set on my having nothing to do with Michael and I didn't honestly think it was reasonable of her. I really didn't know what to do."

The old gentleman looked up at her over the top of his spectacles and studied her face. With a smile hovering about his mouth, he said, "It's nice to have you back, my dear. That curate fellow who came to help me couldn't make a decent pot of tea."

Karen laughed. His reply was so unexpected. His funny kindliness had slotted her back into reality. Her two and a half months in the West Indies would have to become a treasured memory, a memory which, with time, she hoped would mellow and the unpleasant bits would fade, leaving the pleasant ones to grow and blossom just as the lovely trees on Bucare had done.

She went into the little back room and filled the old aluminium kettle, even though she was once again walking across the terrace of the house on the hill, but when the kettle was boiling she knew it was only a dream.

But if only I could see him once more, she yearned. Then sighing, she opened a new packet of tea bags, took out two and dropped them into the chipped earthenware teapot and poured in the boiling water. Tomorrow she must remember to heat the pot first.

Two weeks has passed, and now it was late June. The capricious British summer had arrived.

Walking to the bookshop one morning, Karen noticed how the sun made dancing dapples of light and shade on the grass verges of the park which she used as a short-cut. She was once more reminded of the extraordinary contrast existing on the small tropical island of Bucare, five thousand miles away.

In her thoughts she walked down over the silver sand to dive into the crystal bluey-green water . . . she imagined she could see the '*Ibis*' with Michael waiting at the rail for her . . . she swam towards him . . . closer . . . closer and closer . . . she paused at the kerb to get her bearings. She had almost forgotten where she really was.

The old-fashioned spring bell tinkled softly as she opened the time-worn door. As she did so, Mr. Arnold was standing just inside and obviously waiting for her.

"When you have taken off your coat, my dear, I'd like a word with you." He went across to his desk.

Karen hurriedly shed her coat and went

over to him. He looked up at her and fixed her with a blue-eyed stare. "How would you like another assignment?"

For a moment she looked blank.

Mr. Arnold's eyes were twinkling as he continued, "Not this moment, of course. Tomorrow or perhaps the next day."

"But – but . . ." she began

"Come now, young woman," he cut in quickly. "Don't let's have any nonsense. It's about time you realised your own value. You did a splendid job for Mrs. Hammond, regardless of the irritation you caused her over your innocent association with Mr. Williamson. He wrote to me and explained everything. He told me that you were in no way to blame for what happened."

Karen looked down at her shoes and wondered it there was more.

Mr. Arnold spoke softly, now. "I am sorry to have to tell you that the lady you knew as Aunt Hattie has died."

Karen looked up quickly. "How?" Her cheeks went very pale. She had constantly feared for Aunt Hattie's safety since she had left.

"There is no need for concern. She died

quietly in her sleep."

"Oh, Mr. Arnold," she said, "how sad."

There was a long silence until Mr. Arnold spoke again. "Well, young Karen. How about it? Are you ready for another assignment?"

"Yes." She took a deep breath

"That's a good girl. Then I'll make arrangements." His head bent to his desk and he started scribbling.

Three mornings later, Karen, her case packed, stood in front of her employer's desk waiting for his final instructions.

"Now remember," he said, "you are to take a taxi to the Beaufort Hotel in Park Lane, and when you arrive, go to the reception desk and ask for Miss Tudor. She will give you further instructions. Now, are you quite clear as to what you have to do?"

Karen nodded. "Yes, of course." She paused. "But can't you tell me *anything* about the job?"

"It isn't necessary." He smiled his banana smile. "Don't take things so seriously, my dear. You will be well looked after."

As Karen stood outside the shop at the kerb, waiting for a taxi, she experienced a surge of excitement. It was good to be off on something new. The fact that she knew so little about what to expect made it all the more interesting. This time she would make sure she did not let herself get side-tracked into any sort of relationship. She would remain entirely business-like. It would be so much easier.

Something sad stirred her inwardly as once again she went over all the events of her stay on Bucare. I wonder whether I should behave any differently if I had the chance to do it all over again? She sighed.

A taxi drew up and she got in, giving the driver the Park Lane address. As they fought through the traffic she looked out of the window at the passing scene, but saw nothing, for her mind was still deep in nostalgia for that distant scene.

The Beaufort Hotel was an imposing twentieth century building with a wide plant-filled entrance. Karen mustered her scattered thoughts, paid off the taxi driver and walked up the steps into the lobby and across to the pleasant-faced girl at the reception desk.

"My name is Warde," said Karen. "I believe I am expected. I have an appointment with a Miss Tudor."

"One moment, please." The receptionist picked up the telephone. "Miss Warde to see Miss Tudor." The girl smiled and said, "Will you please wait over there, Miss Warde. Miss Tudor will be with you in a moment or two."

Karen walked across the sumptuous lobby and sat down in a deep wine-coloured velvet armchair. Her heart was beating rapidly and butterflies were dancing in her stomach.

Miss Tudor turned out to be a soft-spoken middle-aged woman with a kind face.

"Will you come with me, Miss Warde," she said, smiling in such a way that Karen felt she had known her all her life.

The spacious lift smelled of expensive perfume with a whiff of cigar smoke and they rode to the fifth floor. "This way," said Miss Tudor, and Karen followed her along a wide rose pink and cream carpeted corridor.

Half way along the corridor Miss Tudor tapped softly on a door and opened it.

"Will you wait inside, please." She smiled again and withdrew, shutting the door behind her.

Karen stood in the centre of the apartment and let her eyes wander. It was obviously a suite as she could see an open door leading into an equally well-appointed bedroom.

On a centre table was a huge bowl of long-stemmed red roses and she walked across to them, leaning over to inhale their wonderful old-world scent and was reminded of the roses in Laura Hammond's garden that had no scent.

There was a light step behind her and a familiar voice said, "Karen?"

She turned quickly. "Michael!" she gasped.

He held out his arms to her and she ran to him joyfully.

Holding her close, then closer, he murmured, "Oh Karrie! Why did you run away from me?"

"But . . . " she began, but was unable to finish the sentence because he was kissing her, kissing her with a gentleness that flowed into her whole body like a crystal clear stream. She was quite sure she was dreaming.

"If only I had known it would be you," she sighed.

"You might not have come, eh?" He laughed.

She looked confused, then smiling up at him she said, simply, "I don't know. I felt very ashamed because of all the trouble I caused."

"Ah."

"Did you know that Frances was very cross with me for leaving without seeing you?"

Michael looked angry. "I was even *more* cross with you. I do think you might at least have waited until I had returned from Barbados."

"Why should I? I had caused enough trouble for you already."

"Come off it, Karrie. You should know me better than that. Surely you knew that I fell in love with you on the ship."

She stared at him wide-eyed. "But you avoided me for the whole journey – except for the last evening!"

"Your attitude towards me wasn't exactly encouraging. Remember?"

He put his hand under her chin and tilted her face so that she was forced to look him straight in the eyes.

Karen bit her lip. "I was perfectly horrid."

Michael laughed.

"Then I am forgiven?" She appeared contrite.

"I guess so. Come here." He pulled her towards him and held her in his arms again, crushing her to him so that she could hardly breathe and she loved it.

Suddenly he let go of her and said, "Come. Let's go down to the restaurant. All this excitement makes me hungry. Over lunch I'll fill you in on what has been happening since you left."

"But it's only half past eleven."

"So what! I've just remembered that I haven't eaten any breakfast yet."

"Why ever not?"

"You should know."

Now they were in the lift going down. Michael held her hand until they reached ground level and the lift doors opened.

Miss Tudor was standing by the reception desk and Michael waved to her as they passed. There was a look of understanding between them.

"Who is she?" Karen wanted to know.

"The social hostess employed by the hotel. Don't you think it's a splendid arrangement?"

They entered the restaurant and Michael asked for a table for two in a discreet corner.

"And now, my love," he said, as they were seated, "What would you like to eat?" He put out his hand to cover hers. It was a gesture of possession. You are mine, he seemed to be saying, and Karen had not the least objection.

But she was not at all interested in food.

She remembered drinking champagne, but afterwards, she could not even remember what they had to eat. All she wanted to do was ask questions.

"Michael," she said, watching him eat his steak with relish, "*please* tell me what happened at *Tabara* after I left."

"Oh, nothing much." He gave a sly glance in her direction, then lifting his glass, said, "Cheers."

Karen reciprocated, then pursued, "Was there a rumpus?" She was dying to know.

"Let me tell you about it," he said. "First of all I got in touch with Louis da Freitas." He gave her another sideways glance. "I believe you *have* heard of the firm."

Karen leaned forward. "Michael . . . please let me explain."

He held up his hand. "Later. Just listen to me for one moment." He reached across and patted her hand. "As I was saying. I went to see Louis da Freitas and he wrote a formal letter to Laura telling her that he would like to see her concerning Arthur's will. That must have shaken her a bit, I imagine. I don't think she knew that Arthur had even made one. Anyway, he made an appointment for her to come and see him, telling her that I would also be present. Warren came too."

"But *he's* not involved, surely!"

Michael shrugged his shoulders. "She needed moral support, I suppose. But let me go on. Da Freitas asked Laura why she had not been in touch with him when Arthur died. She um'd and ah'd a bit then fell back on the fact that she was unaware of the existence of the will."

"What did she say when she learned that it was me who found the floor safe?"

"She wasn't told about that at all. It wasn't necessary for her to know because Louis da Freitas had the copy." He gave her a teasing glance. "So your secret is quite safe."

"I wonder why your step-father put the safe in such a strange place?"

"I really don't know. It *was* rather an eccentric thing to do." He paused. "Perhaps he had a morbid fear of fire after the accident on the carpet."

"Yes. I have often wondered, since, how that fire got started."

"That we shall never know. Though I can't believe that Arthur would ever have been so careless."

"Why didn't Laura Hammond get in touch with Mr. da Freitas when her husband died? She must surely have known he was the family solicitor."

"That will have to remain a mystery."

"But that's amazing."

"It does take a bit of swallowing, I admit," said Michael. "However, it didn't affect the issue, fortunately."

Karen put her hand to her chest and sighed with relief. "Thank heaven," she said.

"May I go on?"

"Sorry, Michael, but I'm so grateful to Mr. da Freitas for not giving me away."

"Yes, well. Solicitors in general are the soul of discretion." He paused. "Well, when we were all assembled, the will was read. It was quite straightforward. The library was the only thing that affected me. Laura was to receive all other property."

"You mean, *Tabara*?"

"Yes," continued Michael. "Two years before he died, my stepfather made both plantations over to Harvey and me. That was when he gave me the ketch. So that didn't come into it. Laura was furious at the time, but my guess is that Arthur wanted to ensure that the plantations stayed in our family, which meant that both Harvey and I would be well set up for life. But he particularly wanted me to have the library. I knew that because he told me so. I guess he knew that Laura might turn the books into cash if she got the chance. But that would have been a tragedy. He spent *years* assembling all those volumes, even going so far as to install the expensive air-conditioning to preserve them. As you know, books deteriorate very quickly in a humid climate." Michael was silent for a moment or two until he added, "I think that's about all."

"What happened about the picture?"

"Picture?"

"Yes. The hunting scene I saw in the art gallery."

"Oh that. Leonard da Vinci is a good friend of mine. Apparently Warren took it to show him and ask for a valuation. What Warren didn't know was that Leonard knew all about it because he sold it to my stepfather in the first place. Leonard was waiting until he saw me again."

"So it's quite safe."

"It's quite safe."

Karen was thoughtful. "Will Mrs. Hammond stay on at *Tabara* do you think?"

He shook his head. "She has departed already. Warren, too. They have left the keys with da Freitas so that I can have the library moved up to the *House*, and then it will be sold."

"Are you upset about that?"

"No. I shall be glad to be rid of the unhappy memories attached to the place."

"Where have they gone? Laura and Warren, I mean."

"To Jamaica, I believe. Laura has property there . . . from her previous husband." Michael raised his glass.

They were quiet with their own thoughts again until Karen remembered Aunt Hattie. "I was very sorry to hear about Aunt Hattie. Mr. Arnold told me." She hesitated. "I suppose you know that she thought the world of you?"

He nodded. His thoughts seemed far away.

"Is something bothering you?" asked Karen.

"Not really," he replied, fidgeting with his table napkin then crumpling it and throwing it on the table. Then he toyed with the stem of his champagne glass, fingers never still.

"What is it, Michael? What's bothering you? There's *something.*"

"Only you," he said, looking straight

into her eyes and searching for the answer he wanted. "Karrie," he said, urgently, "I must know. Will you come back with me? Marry me, I mean . . . and live in *The House* up on the hill?"

Karen's face was radiant and her eyes gave him the answer he wanted. She nodded gently.

He reached across for her hand.

A moment or two later, he added, now lightly, "Oh, by the way, Rosemary has decided to take her father on a world cruise. They'll be gone for some time. We shall be all on our own for a while, that is, until Harvey comes home for the holidays." He paused. "Oh, and one thing. I've been down to Arima to see Theresa and ask her if she would like to come and give us a hand. I told her that Tracy would also be welcome."

"That was a very nice thing to do."

"Yes . . . well . . . "

Memories of Theresa came to her mind . . . how she had laughed at her bruised face, the way she had handled Aunt Hattie and the funny way she always put on her hat when she opened the refrigerator. Karen did not know whether to laugh or cry until, quite unawares, she was shedding tears of happiness.

"Here I go," she said, blinking through the joy she felt and laughing softly as she hunted for a tissue with her free hand because Michael was holding on tightly to her other one.

THE END

Other titles in the
Ulverscroft Large Print Series:

TO FIGHT THE WILD
Rod Ansell and Rachel Percy

Lost in uncharted Australian bush, Rod Ansell survived by hunting and trapping wild animals, improvising shelter and using all the bushman's skills he knew.

COROMANDEL
Pat Barr

India in the 1830s is a hot, uncomfortable place, where the East India Company still rules. Amelia and her new husband find themselves caught up in the animosities which seethe between the old order and the new.

THE SMALL PARTY
Lillian Beckwith

A frightening journey to safety begins for Ruth and her small party as their island is caught up in the dangers of armed insurrection.

CLOUD OVER MALVERTON
Nancy Buckingham

Dulcie soon realises that something is seriously wrong at Malverton, and when violence strikes she is horrified to find herself under suspicion of murder.

AFTER THOUGHTS
Max Bygraves

The Cockney entertainer tells stories of his East End childhood, of his RAF days, and his post-war showbusiness successes and friendships with fellow comedians.

MOONLIGHT AND MARCH ROSES
D. Y. Cameron

Lynn's search to trace a missing girl takes her to Spain, where she meets Clive Hendon. While untangling the situation, she untangles her emotions and decides on her own future.

THE TWILIGHT MAN
Frank Gruber

Jim Rand lives alone in the California desert awaiting death. Into his hermit existence comes a teenage girl who blows both his past and his brief future wide open.

DOG IN THE DARK
Gerald Hammond

Jim Cunningham breeds and trains gun dogs, and his antagonism towards the devotees of show spaniels earns him many enemies. So when one of them is found murdered, the police are on his doorstep within hours.

THE RED KNIGHT
Geoffrey Moxon

When he finds himself a pawn on the chessboard of international espionage with his family in constant danger, Guy Trent becomes embroiled in moves and countermoves which may mean life or death for Western scientists.

THE LISTERDALE MYSTERY
Agatha Christie

Twelve short stories ranging from the light-hearted to the macabre, diverse mysteries ingeniously and plausibly contrived and convincingly unravelled.

TO BE LOVED
Lynne Collins

Andrew married the woman he had always loved despite the knowledge that Sarah married him for reasons of her own. So much heartache could have been avoided if only he had known how vital it was to be loved.

ACCUSED NURSE
Jane Converse

Paula found herself accused of a crime which could cost her her job, her nurse's reputation, and even the man she loved, unless the truth came to light.

MORNING IS BREAKING
Lesley Denny

The growing frenzy of war catapults Diane Clements into a clandestine marriage and separation with a German refugee.

LAST BUS TO WOODSTOCK
Colin Dexter

A girl's body is discovered huddled in the courtyard of a Woodstock pub, and Detective Chief Inspector Morse and Sergeant Lewis are hunting a rapist and a murderer.

THE STUBBORN TIDE
Anne Durham

Everyone advised Carol not to grieve so excessively over her cousin's death. She might have followed their advice if the man she loved thought that way about her, but another girl came first in his affections.

A GREAT DELIVERANCE
Elizabeth George

Into the web of old houses and secrets of Keldale Valley comes Scotland Yard Inspector Thomas Lynley and his assistant to solve a particularly savage murder.

'E' IS FOR EVIDENCE
Sue Grafton

Kinsey Millhone was bogged down on a warehouse fire claim. It came as something of a shock when she was accused of being on the take. She'd been set up. Now she had a new client — herself.

A FAMILY OUTING IN AFRICA
Charles Hampton and Janie Hampton

A tale of a young family's journey through Central Africa by bus, train, river boat, lorry, wooden bicyle and foot.

DEATH TRAIN
Robert Byrne

The tale of a freight train out of control and leaking a paralytic nerve gas that turns America's West into a scene of chemical catastrophe in which whole towns are rendered helpless.

THE ADVENTURE OF THE CHRISTMAS PUDDING
Agatha Christie

In the introduction to this short story collection the author wrote "This book of Christmas fare may be described as 'The Chef's Selection'. I am the Chef!"

RETURN TO BALANDRA
Grace Driver

Returning to her Caribbean island home, Suzanne looks forward to being with her parents again, but most of all she longs to see Wim van Branden, a coffee planter she has known all her life.

BALLET GENIUS

Gillian Freeman and Edward Thorpe

Presents twenty pen portraits of great dancers of the twentieth century and gives an insight into their daily lives, their professional careers, the ever present risk of injury and the pressure to stay on top.

TO LIVE IN PEACE

Rosemary Friedman

The final part of the author's Anglo-Jewish trilogy, which began with PROOFS OF AFFECTION and ROSE OF JERICHO, telling the story of Kitty Shelton, widowed after a happy marriage, and her three children.

NORA WAS A NURSE

Peggy Gaddis

Nurse Nora Courtney was hopelessly in love with Doctor Owen Baird and when beautiful Lillian Halstead set her cap for him, Nora realised she must make him see her as a desirable woman as well as an efficient nurse.

IN PALE BATTALIONS
Robert Goddard

Leonora Galloway has waited all her life to learn the truth about her father, slain on the Somme before she was born, the truth about the death of her mother and the mystery of an unsolved wartime murder.

A DREAM FOR TOMORROW
Grace Goodwin

In her new position as resident nurse at Coombe Magna, Karen Stevens has to bear the emnity of the beautiful Lisa, secretary to the doctor-on-call.

AFTER EMMA
Sheila Hocken

Following the author's previous autobiographies – EMMA & I, and EMMA & Co., she relates more of the hilarious (and sometimes despairing) antics of her guide dogs.

A RARE BENEDICTINE
Ellis Peters

Three vintage tales of medieval intrigue and treachery featuring the author's monastic sleuth Brother Cadfael.

POIROT'S EARLY CASES
Agatha Christie

In this collection of eighteen stories, Hercule Poirot begins his celebrated career in crime.

THE SILVER LINK – THE SILKEN LIE
Lynn Granger

Elspeth is determined to preserve her Scottish heritage and the Elliot name, but running Everanlea, a large hill farm, presents problems.